Jeff wasn't wired for the sort of connection his brother had found.

Then, as the last woman passed by, she stopped and looked up. It was as if she'd sensed him. Her eyes met his. She smiled, and hell if he couldn't see her dimples from where he stood. If he had to choose one word to describe her it would be *sparkly*.

"That was Michele Cox from Alfieri's." Matt grinned and threw his arm over Jeff's shoulder. "Be real and you'll find love. I swear it."

Jeff exhaled deeply. "Lightning doesn't strike twice in one family. And I'm not marrying any of these women, but I might hire her. I watched her on a cooking show once. Hell, she handled her kitchen with such passion, such flare. Spice and color all mixed together. She was poetry in action."

"You like her," Matt said.

Jeff shot his brother a dirty look. "I'm not interested in searching for love. I just need a chef, and a wife who'll satisfy Dad's terms.

Matt shook his head, his voice sad. "You'll never feel it that way."

"Feel what?"

"Lightning."

A Co...
Plunder (...
bestse...

Dear Reader,

While writing this book, an amazing act of solidarity and strength swept the nation in the #MeToo movement. People joined hands and spoke about hurts kept secret for far too long. I hope this is the start of healing for all of us—women and men—for I'm raising sons and want them to have beautiful relationships. Thinking about how love produces hope and strength led me to the hero and heroine in *A Convenient Scandal*.

Jeff Harper is a television hotel critic caught on tape in what seems to be a scandalous position. No one believes playboy Jeff Harper's side of the story except Michele Cox, a chef who has been beaten down by her world-famous boss until she doesn't trust her skills. Together they'll find love that builds them both up until they are strong enough to face public scrutiny.

For those of you still struggling with uncomfortable or even terrifying sexual-abuse situations please know that you are not alone. Reach out and find support. Good, healthy relationships make each person stronger and never tear a person down. We all deserve to be loved and treated with kindness.

Thank you for reading!

Kimberley Troutte

KIMBERLEY TROUTTE

A CONVENIENT SCANDAL

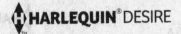

HARLEQUIN®DESIRE

Recycling programs
for this product may
not exist in your area.

ISBN-13: 978-1-335-60348-7

A Convenient Scandal

Printed in U.S.A.

HARLEQUIN®
www.Harlequin.com

Kimberley Troutte is a RITA® Award–nominated, *New York Times*, *USA TODAY* and Amazon Top 100 bestselling author. She lives in Southern California with her husband, two sons, a wild cat, an old snake, a beautiful red iguana and various creatures hubby and the boys rescue.

To learn more about her books and sign up for her newsletter, go to www.kimberleytroutte.com.

Books by Kimberley Troutte

Harlequin Desire

Plunder Cove

Forbidden Lovers
A Convenient Scandal

Visit her Author Profile page at Harlequin.com, or kimberleytroutte.com, for more titles.

Dedicated to the strong women I call my friends.

History of Plunder Cove

For centuries, the Harpers have masterminded shrewd business deals.

In the 1830s, cattle baron Jonas Harper purchased the twelve-thousand-acre land grant of Plunder Cove on the now affluent California coast. It's been said that the king of Spain dumped the rich land on the American because pirates ruthlessly raided the cove. It is also said no one saw a pirate ship after Jonas bought the land for a rock-bottom price.

Harpers pass this tale on to each generation to remind their heirs that there is a pirate in each of them. Every generation is expected to increase the Harper legacy, usually through great sacrifice, as with oil tycoon, RW Harper, who sent his children away ten years ago.

Now RW has asked his children to return to Plunder Cove—with conditions. He is not above bribing them to get what he wants.

Harpers don't love, they pillage. But if RW's wily plans succeed, all four Harpers, including RW, might finally find love in Plunder Cove.

One

Jeff Harper pressed his forehead to the glass pane of his floor-to-ceiling living room window and watched the mass of reporters swarming below.

They couldn't get a good shot of him at this height, since he was twenty-two floors above Central Park, but once he stepped outside his building they'd attack. Every word he said, or didn't say, would be used to bury him—shovel after shovel piled on top of his rotting career.

Dammit, he hated to fail.

Before this week, Jeff had been able to live with the invasion of his privacy and had learned to use the cameras to his advantage. The press followed him around New York because he was the last unmarried prince of Harper Industries and a hotel critic on the show *Secrets and Sheets*. Paparazzi photographed his dinner dates as if each one was a passionate love match. His name had appeared on the list of America's Most Eligible Bachelors for the last three years running. When pressed during interviews, he always said there was no special woman in his life and he was never getting married. The author of the article inevitably wrapped up with some bogus statement about "Jeffrey Harper just needs to find the right woman to settle him down." Which was a big *hell no*.

Why end up like his parents?

He'd mostly put up with the press until he'd seen his own backside plastered across tabloid front pages with the headline "Hotel Critic Caught in Sex Scandal."

Sex scandal. He wished.

He'd been set up.

And the incriminating video had gone viral.

The show he'd created and nurtured was canceled. Everything he'd built—his career, his reputation, his lifelong passion for the hotel industry—had exploded.

Just like that, Jeff was done.

If he didn't fix this, he'd never regain what he'd lost.

Only one person might hire him at this point. Of course, he was the one person Jeff had vowed never to beg.

Grimacing, he dialed the number.

The phone rang once. "Jeffrey, I've been waiting for your call."

Not a good sign since Jeff never called.

"Hey, Dad. I was wondering…" He swallowed hard. This was going to be painful. "Is the family hotel project still on the table?"

A year ago, when Jeff's brother had returned home to Plunder Cove, their father had offered to put Jeff in charge of converting the Spanish mansion into an exclusive five-star resort. He liked the idea more than he'd dared admit. Hotel design, development and management had been his dream career since he was old enough to put blocks together, and he'd steadily worked to become an international expert in the field. But it was more than that. He couldn't put into words why turning his childhood home into a safe place was important. No one would know why using his own hands to reshape the past meant everything to Jeff. Yet…he'd declined his father's offer because RW was a mean, selfish, poor excuse for a father, and he'd never respected Jeff.

But beggars couldn't be choosers, and all that.

"You've reconsidered." RW stated it as fact.

Did he have a choice? "The network pulled my show. I've got time on my hands."

"Wonderful."

Strange word to use under the circumstances, but his father sounded pleased. The tightness in Jeff's chest loosened a bit when he realized he didn't have to beg for the job. He'd half-expected his father would make him grovel. "I'll be there tomorrow."

"There's one condition."

He should have guessed that. Those three words lifted the hairs on the back of Jeff's neck. "Yeah? What?"

"You've got to improve your image. I've seen the video, son."

Jeff paced his living room. "It's not what it looks like."

"That's a relief because it looks like you had a quickie in the elevator at Xander Finn's hotel with a hotel maid. Low-class, son. Harpers pay for suites."

Jeff ground his molars together. "I paid for a suite."

He just hadn't had time to use it while he was undercover exposing a social injustice.

Jeff cared about people and used the power of his name and his show to set things right. The great RW would never understand why Jeff went out of his way to expose the megarich like Xander Finn.

Weeks earlier, Finn had threatened bodily harm to the *Secrets and Sheets* crew if they stepped inside the gilded doors of his most expensive Manhattan hotel. The threat had made Jeff wonder what the man had to hide. He'd filmed the episode himself, and the dirt he uncovered would show viewers how badly customers were being ripped off by one of the richest men in New York.

Little did Jeff know that *he* was about to become the one to "break the internet," with ridiculous GIFs and memes.

The latest one said, "Those who can, run a hotel; those who can't, become sex-crazed critics."

"Success is all about image," RW was still talking over the phone. "Yours needs an overhaul, Jeffrey. Didn't you know hotels have video cameras in the elevators?"

"Of course, I do. I was set up!" Jeff slammed his teeth together to keep from blurting out what really happened in the elevator. His father hadn't shielded him from abuse when he was six; why would he shield him now?

No, except for this job offer—with conditions—Jeff was on his own. Always had been.

"Wait." A flicker of foreboding licked up Jeff's spine. "How did you know I was in Finn's elevator? Did he send you the entire video?"

"Xander and I go way back. He's always been a pain

in the ass. No, I haven't seen it all, but he promises me it gets worse. I get the sense you don't want the public to see what happens next. Am I correct?"

Jeff let out a slow breath. The small digital slice encircling the internet was bad enough. If the rest went public, there would be no coming back. "What does he want?"

"I bet you can guess."

Jeff rubbed the back of his neck. "The recording I made of his hotel."

"Bingo. And a televised statement that his hotel is above reproach. The best damned hotel you've ever seen." RW paused. "Xander wants you to grovel."

"I'm not doing that. It was one of the worst I've ever seen. Think about the people who save for years to vacation at his fancy hotel. No. It's unacceptable. No one can bully me anymore, Dad."

"Then we have a problem," RW said.

"We?"

"Harper Industries has a reputation to uphold and stockholders to please. We can't go around hiring a sex-crazed—"

"Dad! I was set up."

"Blackmail only works because you were caught on tape. You screwed up." There. That was the father he'd expected when he picked up the phone. The superior tone and words dripping with condemnation were signature RW Harper.

"Blackmail only works if I roll over. I won't do that," Jeff snapped.

"Think carefully," RW said. "He's threatening to release bits and pieces of your damned sex video for eternity unless you agree to his terms. With a constant stream of bad press, you'll never work in New York's hotel industry again. Or anywhere else for that matter. Not even for me."

Jeff pinched the bridge of his nose. "Then he's got me."

"Not if we stop him with good PR. It must be done quickly to keep your train wreck from derailing the entire Plunder Cove project. I promised the townspeople their percentage of resort profits and I intend to keep my word."

"The people in Pueblicito not getting their share. *That's* what bothers you the most about what happened to me?"

"The Harpers owe them, son."

Jeff shook his head. Harpers were pirates—takers, and users. The family tree included buccaneers and land barons who'd once owned the people in Pueblicito. RW was just as bad as past generations because he only cared about increasing profits for Harper Industries.

Greed had destroyed his family.

And now Dad wants to donate profit to strangers? What's the catch?

Jeff didn't believe the mean oil tycoon had grown a charitable heart. It wasn't possible.

"Why now?" Jeff pressed.

"I have my reasons. They're none of your concern."

Deflection. Secrets. Now *that* was more like the father Jeff remembered, which probably meant the old man was stringing the townspeople along in an elaborate con. The RW Jeff knew was a master schemer who fought dirty and stole what he wanted.

"You have a choice. Agree to Xander's terms or agree

to mine." RW paused for effect. "Together we can beat him at his own game."

"I'm listening."

"We offer the public a respectable Jeffrey Harper, an upstanding successful hotel developer. You'll again be a businessman everyone looks up to. The shareholders will have undeniable proof that you've settled down and are prepared to represent Harper Industries in this new venture."

"How?"

"With a legal contract signed in front of witnesses."

Jeff frowned. "What sort of contract?"

"The long-lasting, 'until death do you part' sort."

Oh, hell no.

Jeff sat heavily on his couch. "I'm not getting married."

"You can't be a playboy forever. It's time you settled down. Started a family."

"Like you did? How'd that work out for you, Dad?"

It was a low blow, thrown with force. Jeff would never forgive his parents for the hell they'd put him and his brother and sister through.

RW didn't respond. Not that Jeff had thought he would. The silence was a hammer pounding all the nails into the bitter wall lodged between them.

After a long minute RW said, "I'm hiring a project manager at the end of the week. When the hotel is ready, I'll hire a manager for that, too. You agree with my terms and you've got both jobs. Don't agree and you'll be scrounging on your own in New York."

I've been scrounging since I turned sixteen and you kicked me out of the house, old man.

"Think this through." RW's voice grew softer. "The

hotel you create on Plunder Cove will be a family legacy. I don't trust easily, but I have faith you'll do it right."

Those words floored him.

He'd never heard anything like them before.

Jeff stared at his size twelve loafers. He wanted to believe what his dad said, but the reality of who RW had always been was too hard to forget—as was the "one condition." "Come on, Dad. You can't expect me to get married."

"I'll give you a few days to think about it," RW said.

In a few days, another million people would share those damned GIFs and memes. The social media attack would never stop—unless he fought back.

Dad's ridiculous plan was the only thing that made a lick of sense.

It pissed him off, but still he growled, "Have your people start the search for a chef. A great one."

"You want to marry a chef?"

"No, I want to hire one. An exclusive resort needs a five-star restaurant. That's how we'll get the ball rolling. A restaurant is faster to get up and running than a hotel and the best ones get the word out fast. Find me a group of chefs to choose from. Lure them from the world's top restaurants and offer them deals they can't refuse. I'll assess their culinary skills and choose a winner."

"A contest? You'd pit them against each other?"

"Call it part of the cooking interview. We'll see which one can handle the heat. My chef has to be capable of rising above stress."

RW produced a sharp whistle through his nose, the one he used when he was not pleased. "You *must* marry,

Jeffrey. That's my only stipulation. I don't care who as long as she makes you look respectable."

Jeff didn't want a wife. He wanted a hotel.

He needed to make Plunder Cove the best locale in the world, and then he'd have his dignity back. And a touch of something that might resemble a survivor's victory.

A plan started to form.

The producer of *Secrets and Sheets* had hounded Jeff for years to do a segment on the Spanish mansion and its pirate past. He'd always said no. Why glorify a place that still gave him nightmares? But now, his childhood home could be the only thing that would help him reboot his career.

"Fine. My crew can film the ceremony in one of the gardens or down on the beach. The reception will be filmed inside the new restaurant. You can't buy better advertising for the resort." The press would eat it up.

"Now that's thinking big. I like it," RW said.

Yeah? Well, hold on because it's only the first part of the plan.

Dad didn't have to know that Jeff was going to dangle the televised wedding to his producer in exchange for something far more important—the final, edited episode of *Secrets and Sheets*. Jeff wished for the fiftieth time that he hadn't given the raw footage to the show's producer. He hadn't thought to keep a copy and now he was empty-handed against Finn. But not for long. Once Jeff had the recording, he'd release it on every media outlet possible. The blackmail would stop and the world would finally know what Finn had done to his customers, and to Jeff.

No one attacked the Harpers and lived to tell the tale. For the first time that week, Jeff actually smiled.

Michele Cox snuggled next to her sister on the twin bed at the group home and softly read Cari's favorite picture book. *Rosie's Magic Horse* was about a girl who saves her family from financial ruin by riding a Popsicle-stick horse in search of pirate treasure. Michele didn't know which Cari loved more—the idea that a girl could save the day while riding a horse, or that something as small as a used Popsicle stick could aspire to greatness. Whatever the case, Cari insisted that Michele read the book to her at bedtime every night.

Tonight, Cari had fallen asleep before Michele got to the part about the pirates. Michele kept reading anyway. Sometimes she needed her own Popsicle make-believe. When she closed the book, she slipped out of the bed carefully so as not to wake her snoring sister.

Kissing Cari's forehead, Michele whispered, "Sweet dreams, cowgirl."

Michele's heart and feet were heavy as she went down the hall to the staff station. "I'll call in and read to her every night," Michele said to one of Cari's favorite caregivers. "You've got my number. Text immediately if she gets the sniffles." Cari was susceptible to pneumonia and had been hospitalized several times.

"Don't worry, she'll be fine. She knows the routine and is getting comfortable here. We'll take good care of her."

The pit in Michele's stomach deepened. It had taken six months for Cari to learn the ropes at this home. Six long, painful months. What would happen if Michele couldn't pay the fees to keep her here?

"Thanks for taking care of her. She's all I've got." Michele swiped the tear off her cheek.

"Oh, hon. You go have a good time. You deserve it."

Deserve it? No, Michele was the one who'd messed up and lost the money her sister needed. She was heartsick over it.

She drove to her own apartment, poured herself a glass of wine and plopped down at the table in her painfully silent kitchen. God, she felt so alone. She was the sole provider and caretaker for her sister after Mom had died six months ago. Her father had passed when Michele was only ten. Cari needed services and health care and a chance to be a happy cowgirl, all of which required funds that had been stolen by her so-called partner.

There was only one way to fix the horrible mess she'd made.

She picked up the envelope sitting on top of her polka-dot place mats. "Harper Industries," it said across the top in black embossed letters. Pulling out the employment application, she reread the lines, "Candidates will cook for and be judged by Jeffrey Harper."

Her stomach flopped at the thought.

Michele wasn't a fan of his show. That playboy attitude of his left her cold. She'd had her fill of arrogant, demanding males in her career. She'd given everything she had to the last head chef she'd worked with and where had that left her? Poor and alone. Because of him, she'd lost her desire to cook—which was the last connection she had to her mother.

Mom had introduced her to family recipes when Michele was only seven years old. Cooking together meant tasting, laughing and dancing in the kitchen. All her best memories came from that warm, spicy, belly-filling place. While the rest of the house was dark and choked with bad memories—cancer, pills, dying—the kitchen was safe. Like her mother's embrace.

As a young girl, Michele had experimented with dishes to make her mom and Cari feel better. Mom had encouraged Michele to submit the creations in local cook-offs and, surprisingly, Michele had won every contest she entered. The local paper had called her "a child prodigy" and "a Picasso in the kitchen." Cooking had been easy back then because food was a river of color coursing through her veins. Spatulas and spoons were her crayons. All she had to do was let the colors flow.

But now she was empty, her passion dried up. What if her gift, her single moneymaking talent, never returned?

If Michele Cox wasn't a chef, who was she?

She tapped her pen on the Harper Industries application. Could she fake it? Jeffrey Harper was an infamous critic who publicly destroyed those who didn't meet his standards. Would he know the difference between passionate cooking and plain old cooking? If he did, he'd annihilate her.

But if he didn't...

The Harper chef job came with a twenty-thousand-dollar up-front bonus. Twenty thousand! With that kind of money, Cari could continue riding therapy horses. Hippotherapy was supposed to be beneficial for people with Down syndrome but Michele had been amazed at how her sister had come alive the first time she'd touched a pony. Cari's cognitive, motor, speech and social skills had blossomed. But riding lessons weren't cheap and neither were housing and medical bills. Michele's rent was two weeks late and she barely had enough money in her account to pay for Cari's care.

Her options were slim. If Harper Industries didn't hire her, the two of them might be living on the streets.

She signed the application and went on to the final step. She had to make a video answering a single question: *Why do you want to work for Harper Industries?*

Straightening her spine, she looked into the camera on her computer and pressed the record button. "I want to work for Harper Industries because I need to believe good things can happen to good people." Her voice hitched and she quickly turned the video off.

Shoot. Where'd that come from? She'd almost blurted out what happened at Alfieri's. "Get it together, Michele. If you spill all the sordid details, they'll never hire you."

She scrubbed her cheeks, took a giant inhale and tried again.

"I am Michele Cox, the former chef at a five-star restaurant, Alfieri's, in Manhattan. I will include articles about my awards and specialties but those highlights are not the most important aspect of being a chef, nor are they why I cook.

"Food, Mr. Harper, is a powerful medicine. Good cuisine can make people feel good. When the dishes are excellent, the patron can ease loneliness with a bite of ricotta cannelloni. That's what I do. I make patrons feel happy and loved. I can do that for your new restaurant, too. I hope you'll give me a chance. Thank you."

Well. That wasn't so bad. Before she could change her mind, she pressed Send on the video and sealed the application packet to be sent by overnight mail along

with the glowing newspaper articles she'd promised.
Today was the day she'd put Alfieri's behind her and
search for her cooking mojo.

A good person should catch a break once in a while.
All she needed was one.

Two

Michele ran as fast as she could through the parking lot while trying not to break her neck on her high heels or snap the wheels off her luggage. She'd arrived in Los Angeles yesterday and spent the night at a nearby hotel to be on time for today's flight to Plunder Cove. The taxi driver had dropped her off in the wrong wing of the airport, making her late. He didn't seem to believe that a woman like her actually did mean she should be dropped off at the private jet terminal.

Her heart was pounding out of her chest when she arrived at the guarded gate. "Please tell me…I'm not… too late."

"Name," the guard said.

"Michele Cox. A jet from Harper Industries is supposed to take me to—"

The gate opened. "You're expected."

"Over here." A woman wearing a blue suit waved to her. "Oh, dear. Your cheeks are pink. Come, there's ice water inside the private suite but there's no time for a shower. Mr. Harper is ready to leave."

Her first thought was *A shower in a private suite in the airport?* The second was *Jeffrey Harper is inside?* She could only guess how she looked after her panicked run in the Los Angeles sunshine. No doubt her cheeks were more scarlet than pink. She finger-combed her blond hair and hoped for the best.

A door opened and Michele found herself in a ritzy lounge complete with cream-colored sofas, hardwood floors, recessed lighting, deep navy curtains, game tables and a cherrywood bar. Five women were chatting and drinking champagne.

"Miss Cox?" A deep voice called out from the end of the corridor. "I almost left without you."

Her heart skipped a beat until she realized it wasn't Jeffrey Harper. The man was handsome—of the tall, dark, broad-shouldered variety. He was also married, with a shiny new band on his left finger. Other than that, she had no idea who he was or why he knew her name.

"Sorry!" And…there went the wheel on her luggage. She grabbed the suitcase by the handle and kept hustling toward him. "Thanks for waiting. The International Wing was full of people and—" Her heel broke and she nearly twisted her ankle. "Shoot!"

"The International Wing? That's a good mile. You ran that whole way?"

"Only one?" She struggled to catch her breath. "Felt like two."

"Let me take that." He handed her luggage to an agent while she collected her broken heel.

She scanned the room. When she saw a beautiful woman speaking French over by the bar, her heart plummeted. It was Chef Suzette Monteclaire, the queen of French cuisine. What was she doing in the Harpers' private suite?

"Now that we're all here." The man raised his voice above the chatter. "Let me introduce myself. I'm Matt Harper, Jeff's brother and your pilot to Plunder Cove. Before we get on the jet, do you have any questions?"

The women looked at each other. A bad feeling slithered into her belly. Michele raised her finger.

"Yes, Miss Cox?"

"Are we *all* applying for the chef job?"

Matt shrugged. "Looks like it."

"I don't understand. I thought there was only one position open."

"Me, too," another woman agreed. "Why are we all here?"

A woman in the center of the group chuckled. She had thick dark hair and hooded green eyes. "Isn't it obvious? It's a contest. The winner gets to work for sexy Jeffrey Harper." She winked at Matt.

"Is this part of his show? I have not seen this on *Secrets and Sheets*," a soft-spoken woman said. Michele thought she was Lily Snow, the chef from Manhattan's upscale Chinese restaurant—The China Lily.

"He's creating a cooking show, no?" another woman asked, in a Swedish accent. Her hair was strikingly white-blond. Her large eyes were like sapphires against a milky pale complexion. She was tall, svelte and gorgeous. Everything about her screamed perfection and wealth. Lots of wealth.

Michele tried to inconspicuously wipe the sweat off

her upper lip. Jeffrey Harper was going to turn her misery into a cooking show. Would she be able to pretend she was the chef she used to be not just for him but with all of America watching?

Matt shook his head. "I don't know what the hell this is, I'm only supposed to fly you all into Plunder Cove. If this is not what you signed up for, I'll give you the chance to back out gracefully. I'll arrange for a driver to take you back to your terminal and I will pay for your return flight."

Seeing all the talent in the room, Michele's legs twitched to start running back to New York. But she needed this—for Cari, for herself.

She didn't move. None of the other women did either.

"No takers?" Matt shrugged. "Right. Follow me to the jet."

Three hours later, a stretch limousine filled with six chef candidates turned up a long lane. Beautiful purple-flowered trees lined a wide driveway. Michele had never seen trees like that before.

"There it is!" One of the women squealed. "Casa Larga."

Michele looked through the tinted car window and saw a mansion straight out of a magazine spread. It was way bigger in real life. Imposing.

The women all started talking at once—something about Jeff's sister being Yogi to the stars—but Michele could only swallow hard. Why did she think she belonged here with these famous chefs and celebrities? She should've listened to Matt Harper and walked away gracefully. On her broken heel with her broken luggage.

"Jeff is a seriously hot man," one of the ladies said.

Michele didn't disagree but what did it matter? She didn't want to be hit on. And she didn't want a playboy or an arrogant critic for a boss. She needed Jeffrey to hire her and stay out of her kitchen. It hadn't gotten past her that Jeffrey Harper was only interviewing women. Why wasn't there a male chef candidate in the bunch?

The limo parked and the women piled out.

"Welcome to Casa Larga at Plunder Cove," a woman wearing a yellow skirt said in a voice that was soft, melodious. "I'm Jeff's sister, Chloe Harper. It's my job to get you settled inside. You'll be sharing. Two ladies to each room tonight. Tomorrow…well, we'll see how it all plays out. Follow me and I'll give you the tour."

They walked through large double doors and into a huge entryway. Michele looked up at the largest chandelier she'd ever seen.

Chloe continued, "I'll give you a schedule for when you will be called to the kitchen to cook a meal. It should be a signature dish that highlights what you do best."

The woman with the white-blond hair held up a perfectly manicured finger. Michele had learned her name was Freja. "Wardrobe and makeup, first, eh? My fans will be seeing me in Sweden. They can vote, too, no?"

An avalanche of panic made Michele's limbs weak. She hadn't suspected this would be a competition, much less a televised one. She didn't know if she could cook a masterpiece and if she failed with the entire world watching, her career would be over.

Chloe looked startled. "This is not a reality show, it's a competition. At the end, Jeff will choose one of you as his chef. Fans will not be voting."

Michele's heart started to beat normally again until

Chloe went on to add, "We'll have a television crew in here once the restaurant is completed. Whomever Jeff chooses should expect lots of cameras that day."

Even knowing that, Michele wanted to be the chosen one. She had to be. This job was the path to financial stability, the only way she knew to make sure Cari was healthy and happy. It was the kick in the backside that she desperately needed. She had to convince Jeffrey Harper that she was the right one for the job. Somehow, she had to get her cooking mojo back.

Jeff stood shoulder-to-shoulder with Matt on the upstairs landing and watched Chloe lead the women through the downstairs corridor. They all had one thing in common—they were fantastic chefs. That's all he really cared about.

"You sure about this plan, bro?" Matt asked. "You're getting married when the restaurant is done?"

Jeff grimaced. "I don't have much of a choice. That's the deal."

"You and Dad are big on deals. It's stupid. Marriage is not a business contract. When it's right, you connect on a deep level, deeper than you'll believe. Julia touches me in places I didn't know existed."

"Sounds like good sex to me."

"Shut up." Matt socked him in the shoulder. "You should give yourself a chance to find love, man. That's all I'm saying."

Jeff could take all the time in the world, but he'd never find the sort of connection Matt had found with his wife, Julia. Jeff wasn't wired for it.

The chefs walked below him, a slow parade of beauty and talent, chatting as they went. They seemed oblivious to him standing above them. He was fine with that. He really didn't want to make contact until he judged their dishes. Why waste time with small talk if he wasn't impressed with their culinary skills?

As the last woman passed by, she stopped and looked up as if she'd sensed him. Her eyes met his. She tipped her head to the side slightly, and the light on the chandelier sparkled like diamonds across her long blond hair.

She raised one hand.

He raised his in return.

She smiled and hell if he couldn't see her dimples from where he stood. It was the purest sight he'd ever seen. If he had to choose one word to describe her in that moment it would be *sparkly.*

All too quickly she turned and hustled to catch up with Chloe's tour. She was gone two full beats before he looked away.

Matt thumped him on the head. "Earth to Jeff."

Jeff turned to face his brother. "Was she limping?"

"Did you not hear a word I said? That's what I was telling you, yes, she's limping because she broke her shoe running to catch our jet."

Jeff was still thinking about her smile. Can't fake dimples like that, right?

"She ran at least a mile in those high heels. I don't know about the other women in this competition, but that one has strength. A backbone." And then Matt butchered a handful of Spanish words.

"What?"

Matt grinned. "Good, huh? My wife is teaching me Spanish. It means 'she has the heart of a bull.'"

"You like saying that word, don't you?"

Matt tipped his head. "Which one?"

"Wife."

Matt had that look on his face—the "sneaking cookies and eating them in bed before Mom caught him" look. "Oh, yeah. You could enjoy saying the word, too, if you allowed yourself to find the right lady. You don't let anyone get close, Jeff. Start putting yourself out there. Be real and you'll find love. I swear it."

Jeff exhaled deeply. "Lightning doesn't strike twice in one family. And I'm not like you. Never was. You and Julia were meant for one another, you've known it since you were, like, ten. Another woman like Julia doesn't exist."

"You haven't found her because you need to open up. Show her who you are without the smoke and mirrors. No stage lighting. No props. Just two real people being…normal."

Did he want normal? What did it even mean?

"You could start with the lady you were making googoo eyes at. Along with her backbone, and pretty face, there's something sweet about Michele Cox."

"That was Michele Cox from Alfieri's? She made me one of the best chicken cacciatore dishes I've ever tasted. I still have daydreams about that chicken."

"Can I pick 'em or what?" Matt grinned and threw his arm over Jeff's shoulder.

"You've got it wrong. I'm not marrying any of these women, but I might hire Cox. I watched her on a cooking show once. Hell, she handled her kitchen with such passion, such flair. Spice and color all mixed together. I've never seen anything like it. She was poetry in action."

Matt cocked his head. "Poetry in action? Seems like you've thought about her a bit."

Had he? Sure. After seeing her on television, he'd made a point to visit her restaurant a few times. One night he'd even asked Alfieri if he could go back to the kitchen to meet the chef, but she'd left before he got a chance. The next time he'd gone in, he was told Michele had left the restaurant altogether. He'd been disappointed.

"I see it on your face. You like her," Matt said.

"I've never met her."

"So now is your chance. Ask her out. I dare you."

Jeff shot him a dirty look. "What is this, middle school? Dares don't work anymore. I'm not interested in searching for love. I just need a chef, and a wife who'll satisfy Dad's terms."

Matt shook his head, his voice sad. "You'll never feel it that way."

"Feel what?"

"Lightning."

Three

Michele scoped out her beautiful bedroom. It had a sitting area, a desk, two televisions, two queen-size beds, Spanish tile and a balcony. The decor was tasteful and lightly Mediterranean. The room was twice as big as her bedroom at home. Heck, maybe it was bigger than her bedroom and living room combined. She opened the French doors and stepped onto the balcony.

"Oh, hello!" The petite chef from The China Lily was sitting on the veranda. "Lovely view from here."

Michele looked out over the gardens below and let her gaze drift out to sea. "It's beautiful."

"And overwhelming. This bedroom is almost as large as my flat in Manhattan."

"Mine, too." Michele stretched out her hand. "We weren't formally introduced. I'm Michele Cox, from—"

"Alfieri's." Lily took her hand. "I know. May I say

I love your lasagna? It's the best Italian dish I've ever tasted."

"It's my own recipe. The secret's in the sauce." Michele brought her finger to her lips. "And your dim sum is to die for."

"Ah, we're a mutual admiration society." Lily motioned to the other lounge chair. "Join me?"

Michele sank into the plush cushions and exhaled deeply. She was tired, jet-lagged, and her feet hurt from running in heels. "It feels like I haven't sat down in years."

"It has been a long day. I didn't know there would be a competition. Did you?"

"No. I might not have applied," Michele said softly, thinking about how the competition complicated her plans. "Do you know any of the other chefs?"

"Not personally, but I recognized Freja Ringwold, the gorgeous tall blonde? She's very famous in Sweden with her own cooking show. Tonia Sanchez, the curvy brunette with green eyes, owns three high-end Southwestern restaurants in Arizona. Suzette Monteclaire is well-known for—"

"French cuisine. Yes, I know." Michele felt like a fish out of water. A really small, unqualified fish. "What about the dark-haired chef with amazing skin? Nadia something."

"I've never seen her before. But—" Lily held up her finger and took out her cell phone "—Google will know." A short time later, she smiled. "Nadia is an award-winning Mediterranean chef in Saudi Arabia, oh, and her father is a sheikh. There's a picture of him and RW Harper taken about fifteen years ago. So, she might be a shoo-in, with her connections."

Great. What were Michele's chances with this group?

"That's all of us, then. An eclectic bunch. What is Jeffrey looking for?"

"A fantastic chef. Any of us would fit the bill," Lily said.

Except she wasn't the chef she used to be.

"If you do not mind me asking, why did you leave Alfieri's? It seemed like you had a good situation there. I read there was some sort of—" Lily ran her slender hand through the air— "shake-up?"

Michele sighed. "You could call it that."

"Sorry. I shouldn't pry."

Michele studied the woman who was her competition and didn't feel any sort of maliciousness in her. It had been a long time since she'd had a friend to talk to. Mom was the person she had confided in her whole life and now that she was gone… God, her heart was so heavy.

"It's okay. Alfieri was—" how to describe the man who'd destroyed her? "—difficult. I couldn't stay. Don't get me wrong, I owe him my career. He took me in as a young apprentice. He was a great teacher, a fabulous chef who took a chance on me. When things were good, they were really good. I miss what we had together. What we created." That last bit came out choked.

"Oh," Lily said softly. "You were in love with him?"

The creative genius? She adored that part of him, but the rest terrified her.

She shook her head. "He is fifteen years older than me and so full of life and experience. I was an innocent girl from Indiana who ventured to New York to hone my cooking skills. Alfieri became my mentor. Because I owed him so much, I overlooked—" she winced, remembering the night he'd tried to scald her with boiling sauce because it was too salty "—I tried to ignore his faults. Until things got too intense."

Her throat was dry. She reached for the mineral water on the table with trembling fingers. Damn that man! He still got to her. She tried to wash the memories down.

"What happened?" Lily's eyes filled with concern.

She didn't know if it was the fact that she was so far from home and missing her sister—and, of course, Mom—or because Lily had such a gentle way about her, but Michele felt like she could confide in her. Now that she was talking, she couldn't stop. "I threatened to leave because parts of me, the best parts, were disappearing." Now, thanks to him, she still second-guessed herself every time she stepped into the kitchen. Alfieri's caustic words had dammed up her colorful river. "He apologized for his behavior, promised to go to anger-management therapy, and begged me to stay. Then he offered me a partnership. He was opening a second restaurant and said I could be the head chef there. We'd rarely have to see one another and I'd have full reign over the second location. It seemed like a dream come true. I agreed and gave him my life's savings as my share of the partnership. I trusted him." She looked Lily in the eye. "Fatal mistake."

"Oh, no."

"Long ugly story cut to the chase—he hired another chef for the second location without telling me." Another young woman to idolize and belittle. "I quit and demanded my money back. He said he didn't know what I was talking about but I could hire a lawyer if I wanted. He knew I didn't have money for lawyers. I was such a fool to trust him."

Michele didn't realize she was crying until Lily got

up from her lounger, went inside and came back with a wash towel.

"You poor dear." Lily handed her the towel. "I hope Alfieri gets his just deserts for treating you like that."

Michele wiped her face, grateful for the kindness. Lily was the first person she'd confided in about this. She didn't talk about Alfieri much, because she was deeply ashamed. She should've left his restaurant long ago but she'd been in such awe of his brilliant mind that she'd made excuses for his behavior. As if cruelty was acceptable, even expected, from a head chef.

What she hadn't realized was that cruelty would eat goodness and destroy beauty. It had wormed under her skin, stealing the special gift her mom had given her, and even after that, she'd believed Alfieri.

She should've known better than to put her trust in a condescending, egotistical man. She'd never make that mistake again.

The door opened to the balcony, making Michele jump.

"Here you two are." Jeff's sister stepped outside. "Lily, you're the first chef to cook tonight. Please come downstairs to the kitchen in thirty minutes. Michele, you'll be cooking tomorrow. Good luck to both of you."

Good luck she needed desperately, and she would work her backside off to get it.

Jeff paced the large kitchen.

What in the hell was he doing?

The first two chefs had created culinary master-pieces. He'd personally judged them both and gave them five out of five stars. Either one of the dishes would be perfect for his new restaurant. The chefs were both talented and intelligent. There wasn't anything wrong with either of them. The problem? He hadn't…*connected* with either one.

There was no poetry.

Who was up next? He looked at his clipboard and read the names. The second name from the bottom caught his eye. *Michele Cox.*

A tiny spark zinged in his gut.

He picked up his cell phone and dialed Chloe's number. His sister had come home recently, too, and was helping with the candidate selection. Right now, he needed a clear head.

"How's it going?" Chloe asked. "Ready for Tonia?"

"Skip ahead to Michele Cox."

"She's not up until lunch tomorrow."

He couldn't wait that long. He had to know if the zing in his core was real. "Move her up."

"Sure. I like her. She's so, I don't know…"

"Sparkly." The word left his mouth before he could shut it down.

"Yes! That's it. Her eyes, her dimples, there's a shine there. Do you know her?"

"Not really. Do not tell her I said that either. If her culinary skills don't match my expectations I'll send her home like the other two."

"You're dismissing them already? Don't move. I'm on my way." Less than a minute later, Chloe rushed into the kitchen. "Seriously? Just like that, they're done? You didn't give those first two chefs much of a chance and one of them was Dad's pick—the sheikh's daughter."

"Dad isn't making the decisions here. I am. Why waste their time and mine?" He leaned against the counter, crossing his arms.

"Because this is just another example of how you don't spend much effort getting to know people. Do you ever let anyone in, Jeff?"

"What's that supposed to mean?"

"I worry about you. When was the last time you made a real connection with someone? Anyone?" She pressed her hand to his chest. "Here."

Never. "I don't have time for real connections."

"You need to try or you'll wake up one day, grumpy, old and lonely. There's more to life than work, Jeff. More to relationships than three minutes in an elevator." She softened the zinger with a smile.

He wasn't going to discuss the sex video with his kid sister. It had been more than three minutes, but few people knew what had really happened in the elevator and he wanted to keep it that way.

"I'm fine."

"Are you?" Her gaze pored over his face, her expression sad. "After what Mom did to you? Of the three of us, you had it the worst. I still have nightmares about that night in the shed."

Suddenly, he felt cold, his heart pounding. "How? You were, like, three."

"I remember."

He squeezed his hands into fists. He was not going to talk about this. "I'm fine. You can stop worrying about me being old and lonely. Didn't you hear the news? I'm getting married."

She shook her head. "Not funny, Jeff."

He lifted an eyebrow. "Don't believe me? Ask Dad."

She mimicked his pose right back at him. His little sister never backed down from a challenge. It ran in the family. "Stop teasing. When we were kids, you swore you'd never get married."

He shrugged. "People grow up."

Her eyes widened. "You're serious."

"As a heart attack."

"I can't believe it. This is great. Who is the lucky bride? Please tell me it isn't the one from the elevator."

"Hell, no." His insides shuddered. "No one from New York."

"A local sweetheart? Is that why you changed your mind and agreed to come home?"

He frowned. "I'm not Matt. No one has ever waited for me."

"Then who?"

"Beats me. Got any ideas?"

She cocked her head. "I don't understand."

"The great RW Harper proclaimed a marriage to be so and…" he raised his hands in surrender "…I'm tying the knot. Once a bride shows up and agrees to a loveless marriage."

"No. You can't get married without falling in love. That's…not normal."

"Must run in the family. Doubt Mom and Dad cared for one another."

"And look how that turned out!" She gripped his elbow. "Please, Jeff. Reconsider. I want you to be happy."

He patted her arm. "I don't have a lot of options right now. In case you didn't see it, there was another meme released this morning. It's brutal."

"I saw it." She leaned against his shoulder. "I'm so sorry."

Her small act of kindness tugged on the anxiety in

his gut and made him question whether he should tell her what had really happened in the elevator.

Would she understand?

"You're a good person who deserves to be loved. I'll do whatever I can to help you find your soul mate, Jeff."

"That's not happening," he grumbled.

"All you need to do is open your fourth chakra—your heart space. I'll help you unblock it so you have a chance."

Did she think he was emotionally constipated? Hell, maybe he was. "Give it up, sis. I'm a lost cause. Besides, I've managed this long without love, why find it now?"

"Oh, Jeff." Her eyes were wet. "Managing is not happiness. I learned that the hard way. I can teach you how to let your feelings flow. To heal you."

He didn't want to offend her, but yoga wasn't going to fix his problems. She was lucky she hadn't acquired Mom's "incapacity to love" genes like he had. Damned lucky.

"I've got a chef to hire and a hotel empire to build. And on that note—" he pushed himself up off the counter "—tell Michele Cox to come down in twenty minutes. She'll be the last one tonight."

"Okay." Chloe started to walk out of the kitchen but turned back to give him a big hug before she left.

Jeff made sure no one else was around and then pulled up the application videos on his computer. He played the one labeled "Michele Cox."

"...When the dishes are excellent, the patron can ease loneliness with a bite of ricotta cannelloni. That's what I do. I make patrons feel happy and loved. I can do that for your new restaurant, too. I hope you'll give me a chance. Thank you."

Her voice and words were strong. Confident. So why did he get a sense that Michele was fragile?

He played it again. "I want to work for Harper Industries because I need to believe good things can happen to good people." He pressed Pause so he could study her. Zoomed in closer. There. In her light brown eyes, he saw a look he'd seen in his own reflection.

It made his heart beat faster.

Michele Cox was a survivor, too.

Four

Michele stood alone next to the island in the Harper family kitchen and pressed her palms against the cool marble countertop.

She closed her eyes and silently breathed in, *I am a cooking goddess. Amazing and talented.* And exhaled, *I will create greatness.* And then she threw her arms up in victory. It was a superstitious ritual, one she'd done before big cooking nights at Alfieri's to focus her thoughts. It used to work. Tonight? Not so much.

Bad thoughts kept rushing in. Broken fragments of anxiety looped through her mind like a terrible song she couldn't stop hearing.

Why do you think you can do this? You'll mess this up.

It was Alfieri's voice. She opened her eyes and squeezed her fists together.

She couldn't make a mistake tonight.

Biting her lip, she debated long and hard before she finally gave in and pulled up her recipe on her cell phone.

That's right, you have to cheat. You are nothing without me.

"Shut up, Alfieri!" she whispered.

Using her own recipe wasn't cheating. She'd created it after all, but she usually didn't need to look at it. She used to be able to cook by her senses, her mood and something she called "Mom's magic." Lately, though, she second-guessed herself about everything. Her mom and all the magic were gone.

Michele put the phone on the counter in front of her where she could see the recipes and began.

The sage-rosemary bread was baking and the pan with lemon, olive oil and Italian white wine and spices was heating up nicely. The kitchen smelled divine. She stuffed squid with prosciutto, smoked mozzarella and garlic cloves and gently placed them into the pan. Lightly, she drizzled the squid with her secret homemade truffle sauce. Her special linguine noodles cooked on the back burner and the arugula-basil-chardonnay grape salad with light oil and lemon dressing was up next. Everything looked perfect…except…something felt off.

She had a sinking feeling she'd forgotten to fill the last squid with garlic. It wasn't hot yet. If she hurried, she could snatch it back and fix her error. She turned the heat down and used a slotted spoon to carefully recover the squid from the pan. The truffle sauce made the darned thing slippery to handle and it plopped out of the spoon and into the pan again. She wasn't wearing an apron because all of hers had Alfieri's name on them, so when the oil splashed up, it spotted her silk blouse. The one people said brought out the amber color in her eyes.

"Gah! Thanks a lot, you slimy sea booger!"

"Miss Cox?" A deep voice came up behind her.

The surprise caused her to jerk the spoon and catapult the squid from the pan into the air. She lunged and caught it before it hit the floor tiles. Cupping the drippy squid behind her back, she straightened her shoulders and rose up to face...*him.*

Jeffrey Harper's large frame filled the space, blocking the exit. There was no way she could flee or pretend he hadn't seen her glaring faux pas. The way he was looking at her? He'd definitely witnessed her launch food into the air and catch it with her bare hand.

"Mr. Harper. You startled me."

He stepped closer and her heartbeat kicked up even more. He wore a white linen shirt—unbuttoned just enough so she could glimpse glorious red chest hair—and jeans that molded perfectly to his legs.

The casual version of the man was sexier than the one she'd seen on television.

"My apologies. I didn't mean to interrupt your conversation with..." He cocked his head toward the pan and a beautiful copper-colored bang fell onto his forehead. He tossed his head to move it back into place. "Slimy sea boogers."

Could a person die from failure?

She steeled herself to be the recipient of his disgusted look—the one he used in the episode when he'd seen rats running across a cutting board in a hotel's kitchen. Instead, she saw...*amusement*?

"I wasn't having a conversation with all of them. Just this one." She produced the squid that she'd been hiding behind her back. "He was behaving badly."

Instead of berating her and kicking her out of his

kitchen—as Alfieri would have—the corner of Jeffrey's lips curled.

He had beautiful lips.

"I see. What are you going to do about him?" He kept coming closer.

He was so tall. She had to tip her head to gaze into his eyes, which were an amazing powder blue with a golden starburst in the irises. Simply mesmerizing. It was easy to understand why women lusted after Jeffrey Harper.

She looked at the misshapen squid. Alfieri would've scolded her. *That mistake will come out of your paycheck.*

"Throw it away?" she said.

"Why? Cook it up. I'll eat it."

Her hands were shaking when she shoved a garlic clove inside, rearranged the stuffing, dropped the squid in the pan with the others, and turned up the heat. The pan started sizzling, which didn't come close to the electricity she felt when Jeffrey stood so close. His woodsy cologne smelled better than the food but having him watch her cook made her nervous.

"I don't see chicken." He sounded disappointed.

Did he expect all the chefs to serve chicken? Had she missed that part of the fine print in the contract she'd signed?

"It's pan-seared and stuffed squid with my special truffle sauce. The linguine noodles and bay clams are almost ready," she said, her voice tiny.

He crossed his arms, his body language expressing disappointment. "Miss Cox, the chef position for my restaurant is highly competitive. I expect to be impressed by each meal."

Now *that* sounded more like Alfieri. The condescending tone stirred up her anger. "What more do I need to do, Mr. Harper? Juggle clams and catch them with my teeth?"

His mouth dropped open. She'd surprised herself, too, since she usually didn't speak up to a boss and never in a job interview. She waited for him to ask her to leave.

Instead Jeffrey Harper surprised *her*.

He laughed.

It was a good, hearty sound that rolled through her core, loosening the bitterness inside her. She couldn't help but smile.

He had a really great laugh.

"No, Miss Cox. Just excite me. I'm looking forward to being transported."

What did that mean? The way he looked at her, like they were sharing some sort of inside joke, was unnerving. She didn't get the punch line.

"Chardonnay?" he asked.

"Sure, if that's what you like to drink. But I'd probably suggest a nice light-bodied, high-acid red wine, like a Sangiovese, or perhaps a white Viognier?"

"I'll see what we've got in the cellar." Watching him stride out of the kitchen, it struck her that Jeffrey Harper was not as cocky as he seemed on television. She liked him better this way. Plus, he hadn't yelled at her.

She took the bread out of the oven, wrapped it in a colorful towel, and placed it in a basket. Checking the recipe again to make sure she hadn't forgotten anything, she plated up the meal. Four stuffed squid were dressed with the light sauce and adorned with a sprinkling of spices. The linguine and clams were cooked perfectly. The salad was a lacy pyramid of arugula and basil leaves and decorated with sweet chardonnay grapes. The dressing was another secret recipe that never failed.

The meal was not a work of art, but it looked good, it smelled good, and she was sure it would taste good. That was the best she could do tonight.

She sighed. Good wouldn't cut it here, not by a long shot. The other chefs would be excellent.

"I have both wines." His deep voice rumbled behind her, sending shivers up her spine. "Which would you prefer, Miss Cox?"

She glanced over her shoulder at him. He waved two bottles at her. "Me?"

"I'm not drinking alone."

She folded his napkin into a flower shape. "Oh, okay. Um, I like white. Thank you." She carried his plate to the table.

"Viognier it is." He poured her a glass and placed it at the table across from him. "Sit."

Apparently, she was supposed to watch him eat. Was he going to tell her bite by bite how she'd messed up or how the food didn't *excite* him? Would he throw the entire plate at her head and order her to clean up the mess like Alfieri would?

She glanced at the table and realized she'd forgotten the salad. Another rookie move. What else would she mess up tonight? "I'll be right back."

When she returned with his salad plate, she was surprised to see he'd split his entrée onto two plates.

"What are you doing, Mr. Harper?"

"Join me. I hate to eat alone." His smile was more sincere than cocky and there was something about the look in his eyes that tugged at her. Sadness? Loneliness?

She hated to eat alone, too. Uneasily, she sat across from him.

He sounded relieved when he said, "Thank you."

She heard those two words so infrequently that she checked to make sure he wasn't being sarcastic. He wasn't.

"Eat," he ordered.

Huh. Somehow, she'd scored an impromptu date with America's Most Eligible Bachelor. It wasn't a bad way to go out after the worst job interview of her life. Not bad at all.

He lit two candles and moved them so he could look at Michele Cox's pretty face.

Jeff had never met a chef like her.

When he first came into the kitchen, he hadn't been impressed. There was no poetry in action. No color or fluidity. She seemed stiff and uncertain. And why was she looking at her cell phone so much? Was she using someone else's recipe?

Then she'd verbally threatened her food. That was strange enough, but chucking it into the air and catching it as if nothing had happened? Her cheeks had flushed with embarrassment and her gorgeous honey-colored eyes had sparked with worry, and still she'd sassed him. That took balls. And wits. Two things he wanted in his chef.

Two things that made him want to know more about her.

He cut through the squid and garlicky butter oozed out. He popped the bite into his mouth and chewed, slowly, deliberately. She met his gaze, and in her expression, he saw hopefulness. She wanted to win this battle. Badly. A flicker of something lit up in him, too, though he wasn't ready to name it.

He took a bite of the linguine and the salad, making her wait for his verdict. Not because he was cruel, but because he wanted to savor this moment—his eyes locked with hers, the two of them eating together.

"Here, you've got a little—" He shook out the napkin she'd folded into a flower and wiped a bit of butter off her chin.

"Thanks." She gave him a taste of those deep dimples. Foreplay with the chef. He liked it. So much so that he almost forgot he was judging the meal.

"It's good," he said, chewing the last bite. The second squid, the misshapen one, seemed to have twice as much garlic as the first. Inconsistency was a bad sign.

"I know." She looked at the food on her plate and her dimples disappeared. "Good. Not magic."

She felt it, too. Something was missing. "I enjoyed it. Why didn't you make your signature dish?"

"My chicken cacciatore?"

"Hell, yes. I had it in New York. It was seriously one of the best dishes I've ever tasted." If she'd made it for him, she would've been a shoo-in for the job and yet she went with seafood? She didn't know how risky that was.

"I created that dish for Alfieri's. I won't make it anymore."

"Why not? It was fantastic."

"I'm sorry... I just...can't." Her voice choked and she gulped the rest of her wine.

Was it his imagination, or had her cheeks gone pale? Wait. Were those tears in her eyes?

What the hell had he said?

"Miss Cox, is there something wrong?"

She put her glass down and looked him in the eye. "It's nothing. Thank you for being so kind. I'm not used to it."

No one had ever called him *kind* before. "I'm honest."

She waved her hand over the table. "The candles?

Sharing your food? Your wine? It's a sweet thing to do when we both know I'm not getting the job."

That gave him pause. Why was she trying to talk herself out of the position? "Have you changed your mind?"

"No! I desperately need..." She pressed her lips together, cutting off her thoughts. "I want to work for Harper Industries. I really do. I'm just...this is embarrassing. I didn't cook an award-winner tonight. I'm not sure I know how to anymore."

He couldn't fathom why, but his senses told him that whatever she was hiding scared her. Was she in trouble? "You're selling yourself short."

"No, I'm not." She bit her lip. Was it quivering?

Was she that sensitive about her food? Chefs needed to be creative and strong, bold and thick-skinned. Tears in the kitchen wouldn't work.

"If you'll excuse me, I'll clean up the dishes for the next contestant." She reached for his plate.

He stopped her by putting his hand on hers. "Miss Cox? *What* do you desperately need?"

She froze. Her expression seemed serious and troubled as if the answer was the key to everything. "To find what I lost so I can take care of my sister."

What the hell did that mean?

As he tried to decipher her words, she pulled her hand back and reoffered it as a handshake, "Thank you for the opportunity, Mr. Harper. I wish you luck in finding the perfect chef. I'm sorry I wasted your time."

Shaking her soft, delicate hand produced a stab of disappointment. He said nothing. He couldn't. She had the right to walk away from the job; people walked away all the time.

So why did it feel like she'd just quit *him*?

He watched her leave and drank his wine. Alone.

Five

Michele berated herself all the way back to the room she shared with Lily.

How could she have made such dumb mistakes in front of a world-renowned critic like Jeffrey Harper? One bad word from him and she would never cook again. He had the power to ruin her career for eternity.

Well, if *she* didn't ruin everything first.

She knocked on the door and was surprised to see Lily was already in her pajamas. "Sorry, did I wake you?"

Lily yawned. "No. I am getting ready to go to bed, though. I'm exhausted from jet lag. Aren't you?"

Actually, no. She was still pumped from her time with Jeffrey. A wild mix of emotions—disappointment, embarrassment and attraction—boiled in her blood. She liked Jeffrey more than she'd expected she would, which made crashing and burning in front of him even worse.

She walked into the room and snagged her purse. "I need to make a call before bed. I'll take my conversation somewhere else."

She'd promised Cari she'd read her the bedtime story every night over the phone. She would've done it earlier but she'd been called to the kitchen tonight instead of tomorrow. Hopefully, the assistant at the home had reminded Cari that Michele might be calling later than usual. Cari couldn't tell time, but she'd have a sense that it was late in New York.

"Before you go..." Lily sat on her bed. "Please tell me how your interview went. I was confused by mine."

"Why? What happened?" Michele came and sat on the bed, facing Lily. "Didn't he like your cuisine?"

"Oh, yes. He said it was excellent. The best dim sum he'd ever tasted."

A sharp spike of jealousy pricked Michele's insides. *Excellent.* Not *good.*

That proved it. Jeffrey hated her squid.

"What's confusing about that?" Michele asked. "Sounds like you impressed him."

"During my interview, Jeffrey was... I don't want to say cold, exactly. But very businesslike, almost as if his heart wasn't in it. He only asked me one personal question and then thanked me and left."

Jeffrey hadn't been cold during her interview. Remembering the way he'd smiled at her still made Michele warm and tingly. "Didn't he invite you to eat with him in the dining room?"

Lily's brown eyes widened. "No. He ate over the sink in the kitchen. Didn't even sit down. He didn't want me to leave until he was finished and then he excused me. He asked you to join him for dinner?"

"Oh, well, he must've felt sorry for me. I really bombed my dish."

"Jeffrey doesn't give me the impression that he'd feel sorry for anyone creating unsatisfactory cuisine. Incompetent service seems to really annoy him on the show."

Michele thought about it. Lily was right. The guy she'd watched on TV would've asked her to leave the moment she'd showed him the deformed squid in her palm. Alfieri would have thrown whatever was in his hand at her and ordered her out of his kitchen.

More confused than before, Michele hoisted the purse with the book inside over her shoulder. "I'm going to make that call. I won't wake you when I come in."

Angel Mendoza was the only woman RW Harper loved, the only one he couldn't keep. He poured champagne into her favorite crystal flute and seltzer into his own mug.

He'd stopped drinking the moment she'd come into his life. He needed to be alert, awake. He needed to not slip back into that nightmarish hole she'd dragged him out of. It was as if she'd fashioned a new heart for him out of dead, tattered tissue, and was teaching it how to beat. How to feel.

She'd come to him as a therapist, and her therapy had saved his life. Now he was doing everything possible to keep from screwing it all up. He had to make sure that she could live her life, too.

He joined her on the balcony. "To you," he said, handing her the flute.

Turning her face away from the orange-pink sunset, she melted him with her deep brown eyes. Damn, Angel was gorgeous. Sundowners with her were his favorite evening ritual, one he would sorely miss if she left him.

When she left him. Again.

He knew they were sharing a slice of borrowed time. It had taken a lot of coaxing to bring her back two months ago, and he suspected she'd given in only to bring Cristina and her young son to Plunder Cove for protection from the gang that was hunting all three of them. Her return had nothing to do with him.

Still, he didn't want to let her go.

Taking the champagne in one hand, she cupped his cheek with the other. Her hands were soft and cool. "You are an amazing man. Thank you for protecting them, RW. I don't know what I would've done—" She shook her head, banishing ugly visions that he didn't want to imagine, either. She took a sip as if to drown the quiver in her voice.

Right. As if he could not hear her fear and pain. He was hypersensitive to all things Angel Mendoza. Right now, her breathing was too shallow, her soft cheeks pale, her sexy laugh lines drawn too tight.

"How are our guests? Everyone settling in?" he asked, hoping to take her mind off the past that still haunted her.

"Do you mean my guests, or Jeffrey's?"

"I assume Jeffrey is getting acquainted with the chefs we located for him. Quite an amazing amount of talent out there. I have no idea how he'll choose one. Maybe he'll marry one, too."

Cool ocean breezes blew over the edge of the balcony. Angel wiggled under his arm for warmth. He loved when she did that. He pulled her in tight and hung on.

It might be the last time he touched her.

"Are you sure that's his intent? Maybe he simply wants the best chef for the restaurant."

RW inhaled, breathing in her scent. "How would I know? The boy has no bridal prospects in mind and always loved the kitchen. Can't tell you how many times I found him asleep in there as a child and had to carry him back to his bedroom. It makes sense he would marry a chef." RW didn't mention how much the staff had taken care of Jeffrey when his own mother wouldn't.

"You're still going to force him to marry?"

"That was the deal," he said firmly. "He needs to change his ways. Repairing his reputation is the only way I can save him from Xander Finn. Jeff knows it, too."

"Well, if that's the case, Jeff simply needs to let himself *feel* which chef is the right fit…for whatever he is planning," she said. "He should follow his heart."

"It took me four decades to locate that organ in my chest. What makes you think he'll find his and trust it in a few weeks?"

She smiled up at him. "Because we'll help him."

He doubted Jeffrey would listen to his old man when it came to affairs of the heart—not after RW had so badly botched things with Jeffrey's mother—but Angel was a force to be reckoned with. She was the only reason RW had learned to get in tune with his own emotions. Lately, she had been trying to teach him how to forgive himself for all the sins of his past.

He rubbed her arm, to warm her, yes, but mostly to touch her. He touched her every chance he could get.

"How about your friends? Are they comfortable?"

"From the dirty streets to Casa Larga is a mind-blowing trip. Cristina is still jumping at every shadow. It's hard for her to believe that she's safe here," she said.

Twenty years ago, Cristina had joined the gang because she was a young, filthy and hungry runaway. Angel, who had been a teenager herself, had looked out for the girl until Angel left the gang, in fear for her life. She'd begged Cristina to go with her but the young woman was too scared. Leaving Cristina behind had been tough. So, when Cristina called three months ago, Angel did not hesitate. She'd rescued the young woman and her four-year-old son and now she was doing everything she could to keep them both hidden and safe. If the gang found them, they would find Angel and her family.

Angel would not let that happen.

"Cristina and her son are safe. You've got to trust me." He spun her around to face him. "I won't let Cuchillo find her or you. I'm going to break that bastard."

Angel swallowed hard. "I know." There it was again. The worry in her voice was killing him.

He pulled her back into his arms, shielding her, hoping to prove that he would always protect her. He wasn't supposed to fall in love with his therapist—she'd made the rules clear from the start—but that new heart she'd given him? It felt things it shouldn't.

Even if she left, *when* she left, he'd still feel those things. He didn't have a choice in the matter.

After a long silent moment, he asked, "What about the little boy? Is he scared, too?"

"Sebastian is four years old and confused. Living with the gang is all he has ever known. He doesn't understand why we brought him here. He's too little to know we saved his life. He's throwing a fit to go back home and is driving Cristina crazy when she's already on edge." Angel let out a deep breath. "It's going to take some time."

"What can I do to make him happy? Can I give him something?"

"Hmm. Stock options are out of the question, but…" She lifted her finger. "I might know a way to help both him and Jeffrey."

He lifted his eyebrow. "*This* I've got to see."

She picked up her cell phone. "Hi, Jeffrey, it's Angel."

"Hey, Angel. What's wrong? Is everything okay?" RW heard his son's voice through the receiver.

"I was wondering if you could ask one of your chef friends for a favor?" she said.

"A favor?"

"Our little guest is sad. A grilled cheese sandwich might perk him up. Since the regular kitchen staff is on vacation while you're running the cooking competition, I was hoping you could get one of the chefs to help me out."

"Any particular chef?" Jeff asked.

"It doesn't matter, just pick a nice one."

"A nice one? What does that—"

"Thanks, Jeffrey. Appreciate it," Angel interrupted him. "Gotta go." She hung up.

Angel smiled at RW. "Let's see who he chooses to help that little boy. That will be the one closest to his heart."

"Devious." RW kissed the top of her head. "I like it."

Michele sat on a bar stool and stood the picture book up on the island she'd recently used to stuff her career-ending squid. The kitchen was one of the only rooms she knew how to find in this gigantic house without a map. Besides, it was quiet and warm and just as clean as she'd left it. Apparently, she'd been the last contestant to cook tonight.

She spoke softly into her cell phone. "You're still awake. Don't you know all cowgirls need their sleep?"

"Can't sleep good without my story," Cari whined. "Why were you so slow?"

"I'm working, remember?" *At least, I was.* "Are you tucked into bed?"

"Yepee."

Imagining her sister burrowed under the covers with a plastic pony in each hand warmed her heart. "Okay, then. Let's find out what that Rosie is up to tonight…"

Jeff ran his hand through his hair. "Pick a *nice* one?" he grumbled. Why did it matter? Any line cook or fry guy could make a grilled cheese sandwich.

Hell, I could do it.

That idea sounded more appealing than approaching six women and grabbing one for Angel's job. No wait, there were only five now since Miss Cox had bailed. He didn't know the first two chefs very well, and they were on their way out. He had yet to meet the last three. How could he possibly pick a nice one out of the bunch?

No, it was less stress to do it himself. *I'll show you grilled cheese, little man.*

He headed into the kitchen, but stopped short two strides in. Someone was sleeping with her head on the kitchen island. Long, blond hair draped over a thin arm that held…what? He leaned closer to see. A picture book?

That hair looked so damned soft. He lifted it off her face and whispered the one name he'd been thinking about all day, "Miss Cox."

Michele jerked up, her eyes wild with fear. "Cari!"

"It's Jeff. You're safe here." When he realized his hand hovered over her back, itching to comfort her—to touch her—he stepped back.

He shoved his hands in his pockets. "Was your bed not to your liking?"

Awareness came into her face. She rubbed that pretty mouth of hers and sat up. "Sorry. I had to make a phone call and didn't want to disturb my roommate. It's so warm and comfortable in here, I guess I fell asleep." She pushed her hair back, inadvertently making it stick up on one side.

Damn, she looked adorable.

He took his hands out of his pockets and sat on the bar stool beside her. "I used to do that all the time as a kid. When my parents were fighting, this was the best place in the house to get any sleep."

She faced him. "Your parents argued a lot?"

"Only every day and twice on Sunday. I grew up thinking all parents hated each other and cursed the day they had kids."

"I'm sorry. That must have been terrible for you."

People didn't usually say nice things to him unless they wanted something, like a job or a good critique. None of that was the case with Miss Cox. She'd quit.

And she was different. *Warm.* He didn't talk about his past, but something inside him slipped when her honey eyes dripped with concern.

"My brother, Matt, took the brunt of Dad's fury. It was bad. But Matt was tough and took the mental and physical abuse. Sometimes I envied him because Dad at least noticed him. I was the little redheaded kid everyone ignored. Forgot. I broke the rules and threw

balls in the house in the off-limits areas in the hopes
of breaking something just so someone would remember I existed. God, I broke Mom's Ming." He threw up
his hands. Knowing about rare Chinese ceramics now,
he wanted to punch himself in the nose for that stupid
trick. "Who got punished for the vase destruction? Matt.
He lied to protect me." His hands were shaking. He ran
them through his hair. "Why did I tell you all of that?"

"I promise I won't tell anyone. I signed a nondis-
closure agreement, remember?" And then she smiled.

Those dimples did it. He took her hand in his. Gently,
he placed a kiss on her knuckle. "Thank you."

Her mouth opened in surprise and he released her
hand.

"Um. Why did you come in here, Mr. Harper? Are
you hungry already?"

"Jeff, please. You know my ugly secrets."

"Only if you call me Michele."

Michele. His mind rolled her first name around like
a shiny toy.

"So? Fess up. You hid the squid under your napkin
and now you're starving."

He laughed. "Why won't you believe me? I told you
I liked the squid. Ate every last crumb of your meal,
Miss, um, Michele. I'm only here to make a grilled
cheese sandwich for a friend."

"For a friend, huh?" She acted like she didn't believe him.

"Yep. He loves grilled cheese." That's all he would say.

Only a few people knew about the mother and child
hiding here at Casa Larga and Jeff intended to keep the
secret. Hell, everyone in Plunder Cove could be at risk

if someone leaked the news. And then he remembered Angel's request to find a nice chef to make the sandwich.

"Would you consider making it for him?" he asked.

"Of course." She rose. "Maybe I'll recover a little dignity after the flying squid debacle. Call it my finale. What do you want—the kid or adult version?"

When she stepped away from him, coldness rushed in like a wave. It was a weird sensation that reminded him of the time when he was ten and he and Matt had raced out to the buoy in the boating lane. Ocean temps were incredibly cold that day and it was a dumb idea to swim out, but a challenge was a challenge. Jeff never backed down.

With Matt far ahead, hypothermia had set in and Jeff's arms and legs didn't want to work right. He'd treaded water, gasping for air, as wave after wave dragged him under. The buoy he was desperate to cling to moved farther away. Matt had saved him that day, dragging Jeff back to shore as a lifeguard would. But it had taken days to really warm up. When he was low, part of him felt like a layer of frostbite was still stuck to his bones.

But not now.

Michele embodied warmth. How else could he explain it? Sitting beside her heated his blood. His cells, one after another, thawed. It was irrational and damned stupid, especially since she'd already quit on him, but one idea kept washing over him. Dragging him under.

She needs to stay.

Six

Jeffrey Harper really got to her.

Sure, he was as sexy as the day was long, and smart, and confident and…did she say sexy? But he was also sensitive. That story about his childhood made her heart hurt. She couldn't imagine breaking valuable artifacts just so her mom would notice her. Not that they'd had any valuable objects in her childhood home. They'd had bills. Lots of them. Mom's cancer medicines and Cari's special schools came first. She hadn't had a father for most of her life so there was no use waiting for a man to show up and save the day. If Michele wanted anything for herself, she'd worked for the money.

Making a sandwich for Jeff was a nice thing she could do before she went home. It was her way of saying thanks. It had nothing to do with wanting to hang out with Jeffrey Harper a bit longer. Nothing at all.

He followed her to the pantry, closing the gap between them again. Her insides took notice of the heat coming from him. Or was that coming from her? She always felt hot near the man. There was a slight curve to his lips. Most women would have to rise up on their tippy-toes to kiss that mouth.

"What's the difference?" he asked about the grilled cheese sandwiches.

"For children, I go with the sweet grilled cheese. For a guy like you…" The humor in his starburst blue eyes made her reckless. What did she have to lose? "I'd go with heat. Roasted peppers. Habaneros, maybe."

"A guy like me?"

She tapped his chest. "A spicy guy like you could take it."

His gaze followed her finger and then slowly rose up to meet her eyes. She saw what she'd done. She'd flipped a switch. The playfulness in his expression had become dangerously intense.

She had no business stoking his fire, so why did part of her really want to?

"I can go with sweet." The way he said it, deep and low, like she could be on the menu, made her throat dry.

"One of each?"

He nodded, crossed his arms over that broad chest of his and leaned against the counter.

"Okay, but you're going to want to step back. The fumes will make your eyes water," she warned.

"Then you'd better wear these." He put a pair of mirrored navigation sunglasses on her and combed her hair back from her face with his long fingers. She stood very still and enjoyed the sensation. She'd missed feeling wanted, desired. Something about Jeffrey Harper brought out those needs. She supposed she wasn't any different from the rest of the women in America who lusted after Jeffrey Harper.

"Now you're ready to fly," he said, breaking the moment.

She saluted him and began roasting the peppers in a little bit of olive oil. It only took a few minutes for the fumes to make her cough.

He reached over her and turned on the fan. "Better?"

"Much. Thanks." *And, yes, I was just imagining your arm around me.*

When the peppers were nicely blackened, she took them out of the pan and put them on a plate to cool, leaving the pepper-oil in the pan. She cut a thin slice from the pepper and minced it finely. She mixed it and raspberry jelly into the pepper-oil and spread the spicy mix on two slices of focaccia bread.

"What about the rest of the habaneros?" he asked. "Aren't they going between the slices of bread?"

"Do you have a death wish? They'd blow your head off in this sandwich. Save them for another day."

"You said I was spicy enough to take it."

She blushed. "No one's that spicy. Those things are wicked. This tiny slice and the spicy oil will give the right amount of kick. I promise."

She spread cream cheese on the bread and grilled the whole sandwich in a mixture of olive oil, garlic salt and rosemary.

"Looks great. Can I eat it now?" he asked.

She nodded and took the glasses off.

He took a bite, chewing thoughtfully. When his eyes rolled toward the ceiling fan, she knew she'd done her job right. It gave her a zing of pleasure, something she hadn't felt in months.

"That's the best grilled cheese sandwich I've ever tasted." Two seconds later, he went in search of water. "Spicy."

"Told you."

He took another bite. The sounds he made while he ate could have come from an X-rated movie. Wickedly, she wondered what sounds he'd made in the filming of the elevator video.

"I'll leave you to enjoy it." She made the second sandwich with mild cheddar cheese, grape jelly and plain white bread. He watched her every move.

"My sister loves this sandwich. Sans the crust of course." Carefully, she sliced off the edges.

"She's the one you were reading to. Cari, is it?"

Michele nearly cut her finger. "Yes. How did you know?"

"You said her name in your sleep."

"Huh."

He leaned over and pointed at the bread. "You missed a spot."

"Sometimes I leave a spot, you know for the pain-in-the-neck critic." She smiled at him.

"Great. Thanks. Go on."

"You don't take an exception to my description?"

"Nope. Entirely accurate."

She shook her head, smiling. Who knew making sandwiches could be so much fun? It had been weeks since she'd been this comfortable in a kitchen. It felt good. Right.

"Now for every kid's favorite. You'd better come a little closer. This is the tricky part."

"An apple?" He put his hand on her shoulder, as he leaned in. His breath lifted the hair on her neck, sending a shiver up her spine. Her core heated up shamelessly.

"You see an apple? I see a jolly red apple man." She picked up a knife.

Out of nowhere, uncertainty struck again. *You're going to mess this up in front of him. You can't cook anymore. Not without me.* Alfieri's voice was back. Her hand shook just a bit when she held the knife above the apple.

"Michele." Jeff's voice drew her gaze to him. "What's wrong?"

"I'm a mess." She put the knife down. "I shouldn't have applied for this job. You don't want me for your chef."

She turned away so she wouldn't witness the disgust on his face. Or whatever his reaction would be to her admission. Jeffrey Harper was not the kind of man who put up with weakness or failure.

"Relax," he said softly, without an ounce of his cocky television voice. "You're not being judged now. Just breathe. Let it out slowly."

She exhaled.

"That's what I do when the nerves catch up with me on the show. Again. Deep inhale."

She did as told.

"This time with the exhale say, 'This is what I do best. I'm going to kill this sonofabitch apple.'"

That did it. She laughed out loud.

He grinned. "Go get it, tiger."

Still chuckling, she picked up the apple and began carving the first eye. She made a pupil and even added a starburst to the iris. "You get nervous on the show?"

"The more nerves, the better the show." He leaned closer. "That's an eye! Amazing, Miss Cox."

"Michele," she reminded him.

The excitement in his voice delighted her. He liked it. She went to work on the other one as Jeffrey stood beside her. Pushing on, she used a piece of red apple skin to roll up into a nose. Carefully, she cut out a smiling mouth with sweet full lips. After adding the apple stem hat, it was done.

"I did this once for my sister so she'd eat her lunch. Now, she wants all her apples to become jolly red men." She placed it in his hand. "I hope your friend enjoys it."

"That's unbelievable." He turned it in his hand as if it was art. "I've never seen anything like it."

The words of encouragement were a balm to her damaged heart. No boss had said anything like that to her in...well, she couldn't remember.

Critical words were more common in Alfieri's kitchen than compliments. He was a powerful head chef who'd used despicable behavior and abuse to "train" her to become one of the best chefs in New York, second only to him. In truth, he'd ruined her.

She closed her eyes and blocked out Alfieri's angry eyes, his shaking finger, the cruel turn of his lips.

"Michele." She opened her eyes to see Jeffrey leaning in close, studying her. "I don't know what problems you're having, but you should trust your talent. You are amazing."

That did it.

She rose up on her tippy-toes and kissed his spicy lips.

Michele Cox was full of surprises. Funny, sexy, sweet, kind, smart and...insecure. That last one didn't match up with the rest of her personality. Something bad had happened to her, he was sure of it. He wished he knew what it was and how to fix it.

Without a word, she rose up and softly, gently, pressed her lips to his. Fully unprepared, he stood still, cautious after what had happened in the elevator. Given one more moment, he would have swept her up in his arms and deepened that sweet kiss. But before he could, she stepped back.

"Sorry." Her beautiful golden-brown eyes were wide with…what? Had she surprised herself, too? "That was unprofessional. I don't normally…" She was pressing her hand to her lips. "I'll just leave. Good luck!"

Before he could stop her, Michele Cox rushed through the kitchen door and out of his life. Again.

Seven

Michele awoke with the sense that something was wrong. It was the same feeling she'd opened her eyes to every morning since she'd left Alfieri's. This morning was worse.

All night, her mind did the play-by-play critique of every mistake she'd made in front of Jeffrey Harper. Including that kiss. She pulled the pillow over her head in embarrassment. He must've thought she'd lost her mind.

What was that sound? She lifted the pillow, pushed the hair out of her eyes and listened. Sniffling? Sitting up, she noticed Lily's bed was empty.

Tying her robe around her, Michele followed the soft sounds to the closed bathroom door. She knocked lightly. "Lily? Are you okay?"

The door opened. Lily held a tissue to her nose. "He doesn't want me. I've been asked to pack my bags and go home."

"No. When?"

"I was doing my early morning Tai Chi in the gardens and Chloe joined me for what she called sunrise meditation and yoga. After we were both finished, she gave me the news. She was nice about it."

"Oh. I'm sorry, Lily." Michele's heart sank. She really liked Lily. Since they were both New Yorkers, and had bonded quickly, Michele had hoped her new-found friend would win the competition. Jeffrey deserved to have such a kind chef working for him. "Maybe we can call a taxi and leave together. Let me pack up and—"

"Miss Cox?" Chloe called to her from the doorway. "You've been asked to join the remaining chefs in the great hall to discuss today's schedule and what happens in the next stage of the competition."

Lily shot her a surprised look. No one was more shocked than Michele.

"Um, I think there's been a mistake. I quit the competition yesterday," Michele said.

Chloe turned her head and her long blond braid fell over her shoulder. "You don't want to be here?"

Oh, she wanted to stay. Desperately. The bonus money alone would save her. And cooking those grilled cheese sandwiches was the first time she'd felt like herself in the kitchen in a long while. Plus, there was a gorgeous, redheaded hunk she liked, more than she dared tell his sister, more than she wanted to think about. She'd kissed him for goodness sake! That's why she should bow out gracefully before she made a bigger fool of herself in front of him.

"I don't deserve to be here with these other great chefs," she muttered.

Chloe smiled. "My brother disagrees. You impressed him last night."

When? Based on her performance with the squid, she wouldn't hire her; would he?

"It is up to you, Miss Cox. If you want to leave, we'll make the arrangements for your flight back to New York. No problem. Jeff wants you to be happy with your choice, whatever it may be. The other chefs are gathering in the great hall. Join us, if you decide to continue on."

Chloe closed the door behind her.

"Wow, that's just…" Michele sat on the edge of her bed. "I didn't expect he'd want me to stay."

"I'm glad. If I can't win, I hope you do. He should have a great, kind chef." Lily smiled sweetly. "I'm rooting for you."

Jeff waited for Chloe to come around the corner. "So? What did she say?"

"Who?"

He gave her his deadpan look.

She laughed. "Just teasing. Michele was a little surprised. She thought she'd quit the competition yesterday."

"She did."

Chloe cocked her eyebrow, a typical Harper expression. "Sounds like she doesn't want to be here, Jeff. Why don't you let her go and continue this challenge with the other chefs?"

"Is that what she said? Michele doesn't want to be with me?" He cleared his throat. *Damn.* "*Work* for me?"

Chloe's lips quirked. "If you want her, why don't you

end this competition and go after her? Ask her out. Woo her. See what happens."

"It's not that easy. She's not like the other women I've dated. Michele is…different." And struggling with something he didn't understand. She needed to be treated with care. He understood more than he dared admit. "Did she say she wants to leave Casa Larga?"

"Not exactly. She feels like she doesn't deserve to be here."

"That's insecurity talking. She's a damn fine chef, just as good as the other ones here. Did you convince her?" He was pacing now. "Is she staying or not?"

"I left it up to her. We'll know what she decides if she comes to the great hall, which is where I am supposed to be right now." Chloe kissed his cheek. "Good luck!"

Luck. He didn't believe in it, otherwise he'd have to ask what he'd done to piss off the universe.

"Good morning, ladies," Chloe's voice echoed from the great hall.

Part of him wanted to peek his head in to see if Michele had decided to stay. The other part of him reminded himself to cool his jets. He didn't want to do anything that might scare Michele off. It was obvious she was conflicted about staying. But damn, he wanted to look.

A workout. That's what he needed.

He started toward the gym to burn off his frustrated energy. It was laughable. A week ago, if he'd felt like this, he would've asked a lady or two out on a date. Now he was trying to get away from them.

"Mr. Harper?" a voice called.

Damn. It was a chef he'd already excused.

She hustled to catch up with him. "It's Lily. May I speak with you?"

He ran his hand through his hair. "My decision had nothing to do with your dinner. You are a fine chef, Lily. I meant what I said. I loved your dim sum."

"Thank you. That means a lot coming from you. I've watched all your shows. Some of them three and four times." She wrung her hands as if she was nervous and her cheeks turned pink. "I feel like I know you."

He pinched his nose. Was this some sort of hero worship? He was no hero. "I'm not that guy from the show. I'm just…a guy."

"No, no. You are a professional. What happened to you and to the show was very unfair."

He agreed with her assessment. "Thank you for your support and for coming here. I'm sorry it didn't work out. Best of luck in your job search." He tried to walk away, but she stepped in front of him.

"You deserve success and happiness, Jeffrey," she said. "Be careful about who you choose. Some of these chefs might be here for the wrong reasons."

Hold up. Lily had roomed with Michele, hadn't she? What had they talked about? "I'm going to need more information."

"I don't have more to say. Just…be careful."

That told him absolutely nothing but triggered his internal warning alarms because he, too, was cautious. Michele said she needed the job but something had spooked her so badly that she felt she didn't deserve it. That flicker of fear in her eyes? It hit too close to home. As a child, his heart had been broken by people who were supposed to love him. Had Michele encountered something similar?

Hell, these thoughts were depressing.

He needed to sprint on the treadmill or pound the hell out of the boxing bag.

Before the cold seeped in through the cracks.

Eight

The next morning, Tonia cooked him breakfast, Freja made lunch and Suzette rounded out the day with dinner. His taste buds were impressed but none of the meals captivated him as much as that single carved apple.

Michele had an artistic flair rarely seen in any discipline. Hell, in a matter of minutes she'd created an iris in the apple's eye that shockingly resembled his own. Michele possessed something he'd never experienced before. Magic? Is that what she'd called it? Unfortunately, it seemed to come and go for her, which was bad news for his restaurant. A five-star dining experience demanded consistency and near perfection for every dish. Betting on Michele Cox was foolhardy and, still, he couldn't bring himself to excuse her. Not yet.

She seemed to have worked her magic on him, too, with one gentle kiss.

When he wasn't judging meals, he worked with the building contractor and crew. The goal was to have the restaurant ready to open in six months. It was an ambitious time frame, but he wanted the restaurant in full swing as quickly as possible so the Harper marketing team would have good news to release, to hopefully counteract all the bad news still going around about Jeff.

Even though RW's lawyers had sent cease and desist orders, Finn was still doing his damnedest to ruin what was left of Jeff's reputation. The woman from the elevator was threatening to speak out as well. Lawyers had been dispatched to her home to try to reason with her.

The universe kept dumping on him.

In the early evening, Jeff took off his construction hat and joined Matt in the guesthouse for one of their brotherly, cutthroat games of pool.

"Married yet?" Matt handed him a beer.

"Asshole."

"What? I didn't sign up for this gig. That's all on you, brother."

"It was Dad's idea, not mine. Forget about a wife, I'm having a hard enough time choosing a chef."

Matt put a hand on his shoulder. "You can end it now. Tell RW to take a flying leap and live your own life. Go be happy."

"Happy. Everyone talks about that, but what the hell is it?" Jeff sipped his beer. "I like what I'm doing here. The restaurant construction plans are ambitious and, if I sit on the crew, they'll be done on time. I like that I'm creating this place from the ground up. If I walk now, I throw away my chance to make the hotel all it could be. RW will find someone else."

And Finn would release the rest of the video and Jeff would be done.

"This is not your only chance at building your dream. It's a restaurant and a hotel, man. You can do that anywhere, anytime. Building a strong relationship, a strong marriage? That's a lifetime achievement. Give yourself a chance to get it right."

Jeff racked the set. "You going to keep chapping my balls or take your shot?"

Matt didn't understand. Jeff's brother had everything he wanted—a beautiful, adoring wife, a son and a job he loved. Jeff didn't have any of that. Might never have any of it. The career he loved was at least attainable, here and now. He couldn't let it go or he'd have nothing.

"Oh, I'm taking my shot. Be prepared to pay up. I'm feeling hot tonight." And as promised, Matt's first shot launched two balls into the side pockets.

Jeff rolled his eyes. It was going to be a quick, demoralizing game.

Chloe opened the sliding glass window and stepped inside. "Thought I'd find you two here."

"Yep. Boy Wonder is hiding out from four gorgeous chefs," Matt said, and missed his shot.

"That's Karma for teasing your brother," Jeff replied.

"Looked like Karma to me. No decisions on a chef yet?" Chloe hitched herself up on the counter.

"Nope." Jeff's ball exploded into the hole.

"Whoa. Take it easy. You want to buy us a new table?" Matt complained.

"Sorry." Jeff glanced at Chloe. "Why don't you choose one?"

Chloe shook her head and her long braid fell over her shoulder. "No way. That's not my specialty. I'm just helping out until the hotel is up and running. Dad promised I'd be the Activities Director once we have clients."

"You aren't going back to your yoga studio in LA?" Matt asked.

"No. I'm done with the fakeness of Hollywood. And I could use a break from Mom."

"Yeah, no kidding. Jeff and I have taken a decade-plus long break. What's she up to these days?" Matt said.

A shiver rolled through Jeff.

"She's on a yacht in Europe with…." Chloe started, and then seemed to notice something in Jeff's expression that made her pause. She shook her head. "Let's not talk about her tonight. Jeff, I say choose the chef that appeals to your tastes. You won't go wrong."

Tastes. Michele's lips came to mind. He shot the next ball harder than he meant to. It careened over the felt like a missile and rocketed straight toward Matt's head. Matt ducked just in time. The ball hit the wall with a loud bang, knocking a chunk out of the wood paneling.

"Holy smokes. You trying to brain me?" Matt asked.

"Jeff, are you okay?" Chloe asked.

"I guess I'm a little…frustrated."

"Just a little? I'd hate to see you all worked up." Matt motioned for Jeff to sit on a bar stool. "Plant your ass before you bruise my pretty face."

Jeff exhaled deeply and sat with Chloe.

"What can we do to help you?" Chloe asked softly.

Jeff tossed his hair out of his eyes. "Either you guys choose the chef or I'm going with the eeny-meeny-miney-mo method."

"I hear they're all great, but don't you like one more than the others?" Matt asked.

Jeff did, but he couldn't have her. Michele might ruin everything.

He had three goals at the moment: choose a great chef, finish the restaurant, and find a wife who didn't love him. That was it. He just needed two women who didn't make his head spin or his heart ache. But with Michele… His head was spinning and his heart pounded.

He was drawn to her more than he should be for lots of reasons, not the least of them being that nice girls like her shouldn't make spicy sandwiches for a bastard like him. It was too much fun, too easy, far too hot. And shouldn't happen again, or he'd really start regretting that he'd promised Dad he'd get married.

Hell, it was Dad's fault that he was this conflicted.

Why hadn't RW chosen male chefs to judge? A bunch of guys would have made the choice far easier. "I don't know them well enough to make that decision yet. And time is running out. Help me, Chloe. Pick one."

She smiled. "I won't choose for you, but I can help. Matt, let's save this poor boy from his misery."

Matt cracked his knuckles. "Yep. We can do this. Who's left standing?"

"Refined Freja from Sweden, toned Tonia from Arizona, spicy Suzette from France." Chloe had nicknamed them all.

"Scratch the last one. She's not staying. Her food was amazing—probably the best of the bunch—and she knew it. She came off haughty and super conceited," Jeff said.

"Yep, she has to go. Can't have two people who are full of themselves in one restaurant." Matt sipped his beer.

"Shut up." Jeff slugged him. "I'm knowledgeable, not full of myself."

"You keep telling yourself that, bro."

"Oh, I almost forgot the last one," Chloe said with a twinkle in her eye. "Sparkly Michele."

"What, no alliteration for her?" Matt asked.

"No need. Jeff has his own description."

"No, I don't. Michele is out, too." He didn't want to diagnose why those words were so hard to say. He wanted her to stay, but deep down he knew that was not a reason to keep her. She was the wild card in the deck, too risky for such an important project. Why was he tempted to trust her and rely on her to make his restaurant great when she admitted she wasn't cooking as well as she should be? Just the fact that he wanted her to stay despite her inconsistencies was a red flag that his head wasn't on straight when it came to Michele Cox. He walked back to the pool table and lined up to take his shot so that his sister couldn't see the emotion swirling in his eyes.

Chloe put her hand on his elbow, stopping his shot. "I thought she'd decided to stay."

He spun around to face them both. "Yes, but I can't let her. She's insecure, inconsistent and I heard she's here for the wrong reasons."

"Wrong reasons, like...?" Matt motioned with his beer bottle for Jeff to go on.

"Hell if I know. She said something about needing to help her sister. I don't know what that means."

"I might," Chloe said softly. "Dad showed me the report. He did a background check on each of the chefs."

"Any reason why Dad didn't show *me* the report?" Jeff

was livid. His father obviously *still* didn't respect him. He felt like a kid again, being ignored by the old man.

"Did you ask for the report? I assumed Dad's team would've researched the candidates during the selection process, so I asked. No way Dad went into this thing blind," Chloe said.

"Oh." And now Jeff felt like a dumbass because he hadn't asked for the report when he should have. He could only blame his whole life being upturned for the oversight. Blackmail could mess with a guy's head.

"What did the report say about Jeff's Michele?" Matt asked.

"She's not my anything," Jeff grumbled but he looked at Chloe and waited for her answer.

"Michele takes care of her sister, who has Down syndrome. Medical costs. Housing. Everything. Her sister lives in an assisted community for adults. That can't be cheap," Chloe said.

Jeff had not expected that. When he'd caught Michele with the picture book, he hadn't imagined she was reading to an adult with neurotypical differences. His heart melted a little.

"Oh, man. I knew I liked her," Matt said.

Jeff did, too. He more than liked her. But should that matter? No. "This is a business. The restaurant cannot achieve five-star status without a great chef."

"Miss Sparkle is not as good as the others?" Matt asked.

Jeff exhaled deeply. "That's the thing. I believe she is the best, or was. Something happened to make her doubt herself. She lost… I don't know…the passion for it?"

Chloe leaned in. "I've worked with artists and actors in my yoga studio in Hollywood who were just like

Michele. Something crushes their spirit and it's hard to recover. Some never do. What happened to her?"

He didn't know, shouldn't care. "Not my business." But that look in Michele's eyes on the application video—the survivor's spark—made him want to find out.

Matt patted his back. "My two cents? Don't quit on Michele so soon. See if she can recover her passion."

"She quit on me." Jeff swallowed his frustration with the last sips of beer.

"But she came back. You said it was her insecurity talking, remember? I'm with Matt. Give her another chance," Chloe said.

The idea of keeping her around another day lit a fire in his chest. It's what he wanted, even though he knew he shouldn't. "Fine. I'll give her one more day in the competition. If she can't cut it, I'll have to let her go."

"Okay, where does that leave us?" Matt asked.

"With three potential candidates. Michele, Freja and Tonia. I'd be cautious of Tonia—she's got knockout curves and knows how to use them," Chloe said.

"You can't fault her because she's smoking hot," Matt said.

"We're trying to improve Jeff's image. It's too easy to imagine Tonia faking it in one of Jeff's elevator videos," Chloe explained.

Jeff's head shot up. "Wait! You knew the maid in the GIF was faking it?"

Chloe laughed. "Seriously? Doesn't everyone? I highly doubt she was a maid, though. Porn star?"

He hadn't stuck around to ask. "Someone hired her to jump me in the elevator. I'd never seen her before." Jeff put the cue stick down on the table so they wouldn't see his hands shaking.

"Jumped? As in a stranger groped you?" Matt asked.

"Don't...want to...talk about it." He ground out the words through his clenched teeth.

He'd been the brunt of daily internet jokes, but he cared about what Matt thought and wouldn't be able to take it if his big brother laughed at him. Jeff's muscles bunched, ready to throw a punch. If Matt so much as cracked a smile, he'd lose a tooth.

"Some woman just..." Matt shook his head. "Wow. That's jacked up. Does that happen to you a lot?" His tone was serious, not at all teasing.

Matt believes me. Jeff released the air burning his lungs.

Chloe covered her mouth in horror. Her eyes wide with shock and filling up with tears.

Dammit, he couldn't do this now.

"Next subject!" he barked.

"I'm sorry, Jeff. I didn't realize what happened or I wouldn't have joked about it." Chloe rubbed his back. "It would do you good to talk to someone about this. If not with us, how about Angel? She's really helped Dad."

"I don't need a therapist." So what that his heart was pounding and his forehead was sweating? Big deal that he had an urge to snap the cue stick in two. He was fine. Would be fine. "I need to work and put it all behind me."

A silent look passed between Chloe and Matt.

"Just remember we're here for you, bro. All the time," Matt said.

"Fine. Can we get back to the chefs?" Jeff said. "You two are supposed to be helping me choose one, not psy-choanalyzing me."

Chloe nodded. "Sure. We were talking about Tonia. If she's the one you want, Dad's image people will do what they can to tone down her sex-kitten vibe a bit for the cameras. It'll be fine."

Did he want a toned-down employee working for him? Did he want fake and surface level? With every chef so far, he'd wanted a connection. He wanted real for a change. Michele and her dimples popped into his head. And then her curves, closely followed by her soft lips. Damn, he wanted to kiss her again.

No.

He couldn't fantasize about the way she sassed him with that pretty mouth of hers. Or how much he wanted to taste the sweet spot below her ear and see if she would shiver with delight. He'd agreed to give her one more chance, but if she couldn't get her act together, he'd send her home.

"Now Freja is tall, regal, elegant and supermodel gorgeous. She has a stellar reputation in Sweden. Her entrées are supposed to be amazing. But..." Chloe trailed off.

His sister's assessment was spot-on. Freja was a real looker and her Swedish venison meatballs were both sweet and savory. "But what?"

"Don't take this the wrong way, but why is she here? She's famous in her own right in Sweden. Freja has graced more magazine covers than you have, Jeff. Why leave all that to come here to work for you? What's in it for her?"

"Way to crush a guy's ego, sis," Matt said.

"She's right, though. And before Lily left, she told me to be careful. Maybe someone is here under false pretenses," Jeff said.

"Did Lily say who to watch out for?" Matt asked.

"No. I wondered if it was Michele, but I guess it could be any of them. Or all of them."

Chloe leaned forward. "Why don't we test each chef to find out their true motives."

"Test them? How?" he asked.

Chloe sat back on her bar stool. "Leave that to me. I'll arrange outings for each of them tailored to give you a chance to connect with them personally, to find out why they're really here."

Jeff pinched the bridge of his nose. "We already determined that I don't make real connections."

"Fake it until you make it. And trust me. This next step in the competition will tell you who you should choose," Chloe said.

Matt grinned. "Sounds like a dating show."

Jeff slugged him, just because.

Nine

Michele got up early and called the billing department at Cari's group home to beg for an extension.

Even with careful fiscal management, she'd come up short. She didn't have enough for the rent. If she didn't get the chef job, she'd have to scramble for something else and fast.

But when the bookkeeper told her that all of Cari's expenses for the month had been paid for by Harper Industries, she gasped. Jeffrey Harper was full of surprises. She had no idea how he knew about Cari's group home fees but she was grateful.

Rushing downstairs to thank him for his generosity, she ran into Chloe.

"Good morning, Michele. You're up early. Still on New York time?"

"I'm an early riser." And a night owl. Working at

Alfieri's meant being the first to arrive and last to leave the kitchen.

"Well, you should relax today. I am organizing individual outings with Jeff so he can get to know each one of you a little better. To see if your personalities mesh. The other two chefs are going to be with him for most of the day. I'm planning something for you that might take place tonight, but that one is still sketchy. I'll let you know when it's all settled."

This was the strangest interview…process? Contest? Competition? "Okay. So, I might not see Jeffrey at all today?"

Chloe cocked her head and studied Michele for a second. "I don't think so, unless he runs into you like I just did. He's very busy. You go and enjoy the day. Use the pool. Walk the gardens. Go to the beach. If you get hungry for good Mexican food, I'd suggest visiting Pueblicito and going to Juanita's Café. Give them Jeff's name when you order and tell them who you are. We have a tab set up for you ladies in case you want to buy any food in the market or restaurant. As long as you're here, everything is paid for by Harper Industries."

Michele teared up and hugged Chloe. "Thank you for my sister's rent, too."

Chloe pulled back and smiled. "That wasn't me. Last night Jeff mentioned he had some online banking to do before he went to bed. He must have paid your sister's rent then. He comes off cocky and gruff, but there's a mushy heart under all that muscle. I hope you give him a chance."

She blinked. Give him a chance? Wasn't it the other way around?

Somehow, he'd given her a second chance at the opportunity of a lifetime and she was determined not to blow it.

Chloe patted her shoulder. "Enjoy your day off."

It was her first vacation in the last five years. And here she was in sunny California, staying in a sexy billionaire's mansion. It was a little mind-blowing. Suddenly she wanted to kiss Jeffrey again and it wasn't just to thank him for paying for her sister's fees.

On her way back to her room, Michele saw Suzette dragging her luggage out the front door. Holy moly! Jeffrey had excused the queen of French cuisine. It made no sense that Suzette was going home and Michele was still in the running. Why was Jeffrey keeping her here? She had a sense that she was dangling by one thin rope and had better figure out how to climb.

Tying up her walking shoes and zipping her sweatshirt, she headed out to explore Plunder Cove. She had barely started down the long driveway when a sleek silver car came from the house and pulled up next to her. The driver, a balding older gentleman, rolled down his window. "Want a ride, miss?"

"I'm not sure. How long does it take to walk to the town?"

"For me? It's a good thirty minutes one-way to Pueblicito since my legs aren't what they used to be. It is mostly downhill. You'd make it in twenty."

"I'll walk, then. The sunlight and sea air might do me some good."

"May I make a suggestion? If you buy something in town—food and whatnot—call me to come pick you up." He handed her a business card. "I wouldn't want a nice lady like you exerting yourself walking back up the hill."

She read the card. There was a phone number on it, plus a description that made her smile.

Robert Jones, Driver Extraordinary for Harper Industries
For Pickup, Call Alfred's Batcave

"Thank you, Robert. Or would you prefer to be called Alfred?" she asked.

He seemed very professional, somewhat stiff and formal, but his lips twitched before he answered. "Whichever you prefer, miss. Jeffrey calls me Alfred. But if you do that, you must request the Batmobile."

Jeffrey was into Batman? She had not expected that. The realization made him even more tempting. She'd loved DC Comics as a kid. She'd pretended she was a superhero who had the powers to save her mother and sister from illness. Michele's mother had made Halloween costumes for both of her daughters until she was too weak to sew. Man, she was devastated when she'd finally outgrown her Catwoman costume.

"Will do. I'm Michele, by the way."

"I know, miss." He saluted her, did a U-turn in the driveway, and drove back to what Michele now knew was the Batcave.

Michele smiled, imagining Jeff and his brother chasing each other through the spacious rooms and running through the gardens playing caped crusaders. It should have been a fun house to play in but then she remembered Jeffrey had said his parents wished they'd never had kids. Maybe this wasn't such a perfect place to grow up in after all. She was honored he'd confided in her about his childhood. It touched her. She had a sense that he didn't like to talk about himself much and had surprised himself by opening up. His candidness and kindness made her want to trust him and prove that she could do the job he needed. The more she thought about Jeffrey Harper—his grin, those blue eyes, his wide chest... Okay, maybe she was thinking about him far too much. But the more she did, the more she wanted to stay.

"What the hell?"

Standing next to his sister, Jeff watched Freja stroll down the boat ramp as if it was a model's runway. She wore long crepe-like pants, a flowery blouse, a silk scarf, a large hat over her platinum-blond hair and four-inch heels. It was the strangest fishing getup he'd ever seen.

Chloe gave him a tiny elbowing and mumbled, "Not a word. Have fun!"

Untying the rope from the dock, he started up the motor and pushed off. Less than an hour later they returned.

Chloe must have seen them coming into the bay from the house, for she rushed down to greet them on the dock. "That was fast. Did you... Oh, dear, what happened?"

Jeff offered his hand to help Freja off the boat. She pushed it away with a huff. Her hat was soggy, her clothes dripping. His weren't any better.

To Chloe, Freja said, "A head chef does not hunt for de food. It ees brought to her!" She stomped past them both in her squeaky heels.

"She's not wrong about that." He tipped his head to get the water out of his ears. "You owe me a cell phone."

"What happened?" Chloe asked.

"I'll put it to you this way, if I ever start acting like a prima donna just because I've been on television, slug me."

She punched him in the arm.

"Ow. Not funny. I mean it. Freja acted as if there were cameras everywhere. She was constantly turning to present her 'best side' to the invisible lens. Hell, if she'd just sat still and held the rod like I taught her, she wouldn't have lost her balance and gone ass-backward into the drink. And I wouldn't have had to rescue her."

He could see his sister was trying not to laugh. "Does she think we are secretly filming the chefs?"

They walked back toward the house. "Apparently. I tried to tell her the truth but she doesn't want to buy it. She thinks she's the only one in the competition who knows what's really going on."

"So...you didn't get to connect with her on a personal level."

"I saved her life and her giant floppy hat. Does that count?"

Chloe shook her head. "No, but it does give us a little insight. She's here for the spotlight. That might not be a bad thing. She knows how to work the cameras to improve your image and promote the restaurant. Her fan base in Europe is substantial already. And she is beautiful. Unless you can't stand her personality, I don't think we should count her out yet."

"I didn't say I couldn't stand her," he grumbled. "It's hard to communicate with her, though. She doesn't listen to my stories and she sure as hell didn't make me laugh." He flipped his wet hair off his forehead and wanted to slap himself. Since when did those qualities matter in a chef?

Michele Cox was ruining him.

"Get a hot shower. You're meeting Tonia at the stables at one o'clock," Chloe said.

Up at dawn at the building site, the morning spent fishing and performing ocean rescue, and horseback riding in the afternoon. Was his sister trying to kill him?

"Fine, as long as I get to soak in the hot tub tonight. I haven't ridden in so long, I might not be able to sit for a week."

He had a vision of Michele joining him in the warm bubbles and shook it off. He shouldn't see her in a bathing suit or he'd never be able to send her home.

"Sure, after the dinner party," Chloe said. "Dad says he can't make it to the California Restaurant and Lodging Association legislative meeting and dinner. You'll have to do it for him."

He gave Chloe a dark look. "No way, I'm not going to that." He wasn't ready to get sliced and diced in public yet. He didn't have a stellar restaurant to speak for him yet and the hotel was still in the planning phase. It was too soon.

"Dad thought you'd say that. He had hotel mock-up brochures made for you to wave around. They're awesome, Jeff. And you are the perfect guy to talk up the resort. This will be good for you, to get out there and show everyone that the stupid video hasn't fazed you. You're running this show, just like you always do. You'll see."

Was he running the show? Sometimes, it didn't feel like it. What happened in that video had knocked him back, but he'd gotten up and was working to be smarter, stronger, unfazed.

Like Michele.

Ten

It had to be the smallest town she'd ever seen. The main road had a few stores, an old adobe church, a miniature post office, a gas station and a couple of mom-and-pop stores. There were zero stoplights. Three roads with Spanish names jutted off toward the residential section of town. She strolled down one of the side roads in search of beach access and passed quaint old houses that looked to be at least a hundred years old.

A man washing a motorcycle in a small driveway looked up when she passed. "Miss Cox! Are you lost?"

It was Matt, Jeffrey's older brother. He lived here? "I'm looking for the beach."

He pointed. "Go back a quarter of a mile and you'll find the access road. Follow the signs and stay out of the snowy plover hatchery."

"Will do. How about lunch? Any place you recommend?"

"Not to your caliber of fine dining, but the best Mexican food is at my mother-in-law's place. Juanita's. You can't miss it."

Mother-in-law? Interesting that a rich boy would leave Casa Larga to marry someone from this small town and then live here. "Thanks."

"Oh, and, Miss Cox? I'm rooting for you."

Her chest warmed. It felt good to have someone believe in her again. Maybe she could do this. "Thanks."

Walking back down the main street, she found Juanita's Mexican Market and Café. The smell of barbecued meat made her stomach growl. She hadn't eaten breakfast and it was already close to noon. There were a handful of tables outside on the patio, full with people laughing and eating. Each table had baskets of tortilla chips and bowls filled with what seemed to be homemade salsa. Michele's mouth watered. Since there were no available tables, she thought she'd have to order a meal to go.

"Hey, lady. Wanna join us?" An older woman called from a table.

"Yeah, come on, we don't mind sharing. Well, Nona does," a second woman said.

The third woman had just dipped her chip into a small bowl of guacamole. "I told you to order your own. I don't like double-dipping." She pointed to the one available chair and said in a demanding voice, "*Por supuesto, siéntate.*"

Michele didn't think she had a choice. She sat down. "Thank you. I'm Michele."

"You're one of Jeffrey's fancy cooks. I'm Alana, she's Flora and the guac-hoarder over there is Nona. We're sisters."

"I like to keep my germs to myself," Nona complained.

"My sister and I used to fight over food, too," Michele sighed. "I miss that."

Flora's hand went to her mouth and Alana made a little squeak.

"We lost our sister once. Thank God she's back for now," Nona said. "May your sister rest in peace." All three women made the sign of the cross over themselves.

"Oh, no. She's in New York. She's fine." Sort of. "It's just that I am used to seeing her every day. This separation is difficult."

Alana nodded. "Don't know what I'd do without these two picking on me every day." She pushed the basket of chips toward Michele. "Eat up. We'll get the waitress to take your order."

"How's the competition coming? I hear it's down to three chefs," Nona said.

Michele chewed a chip and marveled at how fast word spread in a small town. "The competition is amazing. Though I don't have much of a chance."

"Why would you think that?" Nona said.

Without going into the long story, Michele said simply, "I seem to have misplaced my confidence and my talent."

"You should learn from Jeffrey. He's talented and self-assured. Amazing, no? After how his mother treated him, it's a wonder he didn't end up crazy like his father," Alana said. "Those two were the worst."

"*Cállate*," Nona admonished hissed Alana. "That is private business."

"Jeffrey told me his parents fought," Michele said.

"It surprises me that he shared any of it. He must trust you, but I don't think we should add fuel to the fire." Nona gave both of her sisters a strong look to keep their mouths shut.

"*Claro.*" Alana lifted her chin defiantly. "We wouldn't want anyone to know the evil mother ignored that sweet boy for days and screamed at him for no reason."

"That's awful," Michele said.

"A friend in the Harpers' kitchen said she had to make sure Jeffrey had enough food to eat," Flora pitched in.

"That woman is the worst mother ever," Flora said. "She didn't deserve those three beautiful babies. And that Jeffrey was so adorable with his copper hair and freckles. Who wouldn't love him?"

Michele's heart broke. She'd always known her mother loved her. She'd even said so with her last breath.

Alana nodded. "Holy Madre, she is terrible. I hope she never comes back here."

Nona's thin shoulders rounded and she seemed to cave in. "She told everyone that I beat little Matthew. If I hadn't taken the brush from her hand, I don't know what would have happened…" Nona squeezed her eyes shut on the memory.

"Now I understand why that beautiful house seems so dark and cold. I'm glad his mother is no longer in the picture," Michele said softly.

"We are all glad of that. Things are getting better." Nona brightened. "Angel is there to help RW heal. She's convinced him to seek forgiveness from everyone he's harmed in the past. Believe me, it is a long list. But because he wants to change, he has asked the three kids to come home. We'll see if they forgive him or not, but it is great to have them all here."

Michele didn't know who Angel was or why RW needed healing, but she kept those questions to herself. What she really wanted was to know more about Jeffrey. Maybe she could help him before he sent her home. It was the least she could do after he'd paid her sister's expenses.

Michele ate the last chip and said, "It's amazing to me that his childhood was bad because he is so—"

"Handsome," Flora interrupted.

"Strong," Alana added.

"Smart," Nona said.

"Yes. All those things, but I was going to say 'sure of himself.' I wish I had an ounce of his confidence."

"Sure, sure he is confident but he is alone. He needs someone to take care of him, like his family never did. If we could only find him a wife—"

Three heads swung toward her.

Michele lifted her hands. "I'm just trying to be his chef."

She needed the job Jeffrey was offering, not a husband. Her sister depended on her to provide a stable income and life for the two of them. Getting romantically involved with a playboy who'd publicly declared he'd never get married? That would be the opposite of stability. Besides, she was not ready to trust any man with her heart after Alfieri had betrayed her.

The three women meant well, but marrying sexy Jeffrey Harper was not in the cards.

Besides, with all the women Jeffrey dated, how could he ever be alone?

* * *

RW stood on his balcony and looked out over his estate. It was beautiful, no denying it. His thousands of acres of gardens, pastures and grassy knolls all stretched out gracefully to the private beach that dipped into the sea. In the distance, he could see his nine oil derricks formed into a horseshoe in the sea. They were lit up like Christmas trees. Some would say he was successful and had created quite a legacy for his kids.

RW knew better. None of the toys, land or business meant a damn. The only things that truly mattered were setting things straight with his kids and winning the heart of the woman he couldn't seem to live without. And protecting them all.

Angel knocked on his open door and came on in. "Is everything okay?"

"Hell, yes. Now that you're here."

"Your text said come right away." She studied his face in her subtle way, looking for signs of distress. He knew all her tricks.

He grinned. "I figured you needed a break from that screaming kid."

"Cristina's boy is a bit of a handful. But I don't blame him. He misses his little friends and…" she swallowed hard "…the others."

He knew her dark spots, too. It killed him every time her sweet expressions twisted in momentary panic, which happened only when she thought about her ex-boyfriend, Cuchillo, and his gang. She had barely escaped those killers when she was a pregnant teenager. She'd been on the run, hiding in Plunder Cove for years with a secret identity and job as the local Mexican restaurant owner. Since she'd helped

Cristina and Sebastian to escape to Plunder Cove, Angel was thinking about her ex more often. RW would fix that. He picked up the remote and pressed the button. Mexican music started playing.

Stretching his hand toward her he said, "*Baila conmigo.*"

"Randall Wesley Harper! You're speaking Spanish."

Now that look of surprise was good. He loved impressing her. "People who call me by my full name are usually pissed off. I love the way you say it."

She turned her head, listening. "My favorite song since I was a little girl. How did you know?"

"A little birdie told me."

She smiled. "Henry."

"Yep, don't tell grandkids any secrets unless you want them broadcasted." He wiggled his fingers at her. "Come on, *bella. Baila conmigo.*" She took his hand and he spun her into his embrace. "That's more like it."

She felt so good in his arms. Heart to heart. Body to body.

This meant something, though he didn't dare name it.

Angel was a dream he didn't want to wake up from. It was going to hurt in the end. He might not survive it.

Pressing her cheek to his, she played with the hair at the base of his neck. They swayed together in perfect rhythm. He sang softly in her ear.

"You know all the words?" She pulled back and he could see the shock of delight. "Do you understand them?"

He lifted his eyebrow and gave her one of his cocky grins. Jeffrey might have been famous for a grin just like it, but he'd learned the smug look from his old man. "I'm not just another pretty face, Angel."

She chuckled. "Go ahead, then. Translate."

He looked into her eyes and spoke the words he'd learned from heart. "Little mourning dove, my love, my heart. Do not fly away from me. I could not endure without your love. Cannot breathe without you with me. My heart beats only for you. You are my world. My everything."

Her eyes welled.

He kissed her with all the passion in his damaged heart. It beat strong when it was close to hers.

She held on to his neck and matched him kiss for kiss while he ran his hands down her lovely shoulders to her back. He pressed her against him and silently begged her to stay.

"RW." Her voice was breathy. "Close the door."

Eleven

Michele's hands were full of groceries. She'd bought all sorts of interesting and authentic ingredients at Juanita's Mexican Market and Café but had not gotten a chance to meet the owner herself. Too bad. She would've liked to have asked a few questions about the Harpers.

What those three sisters had told her seemed impossible. It was mind-boggling that a family so wealthy and famous could have such terrible troubles. Poor Jeffrey. She admired him for working to become successful after being raised like that and then being kicked out of the house when he was only sixteen. Her childhood had been a piece of cake by comparison. Even though her dad had died when Michele was only ten and her mom had to be both parents after that, she always knew she was loved. Her mother had been the best mom on the planet, even if cancer had cut her life far too short. The love her mother had given her made the situation Michele was in that much harder. She had to be the mom now for Cari and make sure her sister had everything she needed. She couldn't afford to get involved with Jeff or any man until she had her responsibilities under control.

Michele found a spot on the sidewalk that was out of the foot traffic to put the grocery bags down and dug into her purse for her cell phone. Smiling at the business card in her hand, she dialed.

"This is Michele Cox. Am I speaking to Alfred at the Batcave?"

A deep chuckle came through her phone. "Yes, yes, you are. Would you like a ride, miss?"

"I would. Thank you. I'm standing outside Juanita's," Michele said.

"Very good. We'll be right there."

We? Her heart beat a little faster.

Was Jeffrey coming, too?

She expected the long car that Alfred had been driving in the morning. She did a double take when a bright yellow Bentley convertible pulled up beside her with the top down. Alfred wore a plaid British ivy cap over his bald head while his passenger sat in the front seat with her long blond hair flowing in the wind. Chloe, not Jeffrey.

"Hi, Michele. Thought I'd tag along so we can stop at a shop along the way. I'll move to the back," Chloe said. "Alfred, take us to Carolina's."

Michele handed her bags to Alfred who loaded them in the trunk. "Carolina's?" She'd seen pretty much everything the little town had to offer but didn't remember that store.

"It's a one-stop dress store for baptisms, *quincea-*

ñera parties, proms and weddings. Lots of color and yards of frill and lace but I've got my fingers crossed they have at least one gown that will work for you tonight."

"I don't understand," Michele said.

"For your outing with Jeff. It's been firmed up. Each one has been a different way for Jeff to get to know the chefs better. Freja, for example, went fishing with him this morning. And Tonia and he rode horses."

"I've never been on a boat before and love riding horses. Those outings sound lovely."

"Well, they were illuminating, that's for sure." Chloe smiled. "The other two chefs had adventures in Plunder Cove but yours will be up the coast in another little oceanside town just south of Big Sur called Seal Point. Matt is flying Jeff up there for a meeting with the California Restaurant and Lodging Association. There is a dinner party afterward with lots of big shots and some press. He really doesn't want to go to this event, but it's important to get the word out about the Plunder Cove hotel. And let's face it, a conservative dinner party with a respectable date can help improve Jeffrey's public image. All you two need to do is show up for the dinner and then you both can leave. Alfred will drive you back home together."

Date?

She needed to keep her eye on the prize—the job, not the sexy man. Going on a date with him would be dangerous. Even as warning bells were going off in her brain, her lips were itching for another chance to taste Jeffrey's full lips. A real date could be more temptation than she could handle.

"This is an important night for my brother. Please

say you'll help him," Chloe said. "We have to do something to fix his damaged image."

Schmoozing at dinner parties. Talking to big shots. Wearing a gown. All these things were so far outside Michele's wheelhouse that she didn't know where to begin. She was more comfortable behind the scenes and in the kitchen than outside where the VIPs ate. But she would go to this event to prove to Jeffrey that she could represent Harper Industries in any environment and convince him to choose her.

"Just tell me what I need to do." Her voice sounded meek, unconvincing. She cleared her throat. "I want to help him, any way I can."

"My brother likes you." Chloe touched her arm. "Be yourself, Michele. And have a nice time."

Trying not to yawn, Jeff shifted in his seat to ease off his sore backside. Tonia had sucked at horseback riding and had only wanted to ask him about his family—his brother, his sister, his father…and anyone else that lived at Casa Larga. Thankfully, they'd cut the adventure short before he'd had to come up with answers for her, or listening to the governor's speech right now would be even more painful than it already was.

He looked around the conference hall. It was packed with all the big boys in the California hotel industry plus a few tiny fish trying to make a splash for themselves. Where did he fit in? Jeff might be a small fish after having his reputation decimated, but he was working for one of the biggest companies in the world. When he made eye contact with some of the attendees, he could tell he was hated by some and idolized by others. Story of his life.

He checked his phone. No new GIFs. He should be grateful. Instead, it worried him. Had the lawyers convinced Finn to cease and desist, or was he working on the next series of damning videos?

Just then Chloe texted him.

Oh, brother of mine, you owe me. Big-time.

Why?

You'll see. How's the meeting?

Kill me now before the boredom does. What do I owe you for?

Tonight's adventure.

He frowned.

No more damned adventures today. I'm beat. As soon as this never-ending meeting wraps up, I'm going home and falling into bed.

You can't. Dad asked me to make sure you stay for the dinner party.

No.

His sister knew why he hated to eat alone. Eating with a group of strangers was not much better.

Come on. It's important for you to mingle and spread

the word about our hotel. Show them the brochure. Talk it up. Besides, your date is on her way.

His pulse kicked up.

My date?

Don't worry, I packed your tux on the plane and Matt brought it to the hotel. They're holding it for you in the lobby. Have a nice time! Alfred will bring you both back to the Batcave when you're ready. Gotta run. You can thank me tomorrow.

Who's my date?

There was no response.

Chloe!

The texting had stopped. Dammit, his sister was toying with him. And now he had the rest of the meeting to wonder who would show up tonight. Was this supposed to be a real date or was it part of the interview process?

Hell, *who* was his date?

He'd already spent time with Freja and Tonia. Would it be pretty, sweet, kind Michele?

He'd missed seeing her today. She was the only chef he'd connected with on a personal level, and quickly, which made him wary. Plus, he couldn't stop thinking about the kiss in the kitchen. And how he wished he'd pressed her up against the kitchen island and kissed her back.

He honestly hoped it wasn't Michele because he would be distracted by her. When she was close it was hard to concentrate on anything but the light catching in her hair and eyes, and the way her smile crinkles tugged at a soft spot in his chest, the rise and fall of her breasts when she breathed…damn. He was in big trouble if his date was Michele.

Worse. If the big boys at the dinner party intimidated her, bringing out her insecurities, she'd be going home tomorrow. He had a job to do and couldn't make any more excuses for her. He'd have to cut her loose. And that would be the worst.

Michele felt a little funny sitting in the back of the limo while Alfred drove, but he said he wouldn't have it any other way. "You look like a movie star, Miss Cox. And you'll be treated like one tonight. You just relax. The drive up the coastal highway is beautiful."

He wasn't kidding. The highway meandered and curved along the blue-green craggy-rocked Pacific Ocean. It was breathtaking.

"And here we are. Seal Point," Alfred said, as he pulled up to the lobby of a two-story building.

She'd expected something larger, more ornate, and was pleasantly surprised by the rustic wood-sided lodge atop the rocky cliffs. Torches lit pathways through gardens and into groves of lacy dark green Monterey pines. It felt intimate, somehow. The sun was an orange ball of wax melting into the Pacific Ocean. The sea breeze softly caressed her skin. It was a beautiful night, fragrant and warm. The setting was so romantic. And inside the lodge was the man who had the power to make her professional dreams come true and tempt her into destroying everything. She wanted him and knew she shouldn't act on her desires.

Alfred opened her door. "Ready, miss?"

As I'll ever be.

She'd never had her makeup professionally done before today, nor her hair swept up so perfectly. The dress Chloe had purchased for her was pale pink and clung to her curves like a cloud.

For the first time since she'd left her hometown to work for Alfieri, Michele felt beautiful. Special. Even if it was just a fantasy for tonight. She was at a stunningly romantic place, but she wasn't here for romance. It was her job to make Jeffrey Harper look respectable, which meant she wasn't going to gaze into his pretty starburst blues or let his deep voice delight her, and she was certainly not going to kiss his full lips.

This was a business dinner, nothing more. She could do this because Jeffrey needed her. And if she proved capable here, perhaps he'd choose her for his restaurant.

You'll fail like you always do. You'll embarrass Jeffrey in front of everyone.

"Shut up, Alfieri!" she mumbled under her breath.

"Miss? Did you say something?" Alfred still stood by the door waiting for her to get out.

Her legs seemed unable to move. "If I asked you to drive me back to the Batcave, would you do it?" Her voice was shaky.

Alfred leaned closer and whispered, "Is that what you want, miss?"

If I leave now, I might as well fly straight home to New York.

She swallowed. "No. I'm just a little nervous. I'm not used to parties like this." Or being on a date with a famous, wealthy man. Who was she kidding? Any man. She hadn't been on a date in years. "Where do I go?"

"I believe the people in the lobby can direct you to the restaurant where the dinner party is taking place."

She nodded. "Sure, okay."

"Miss Cox? I'll be out here waiting for you and Jeffrey. Say the word and I will drive you back to Plunder Cove. But I believe you will be great tonight. Do as Chloe said and simply be yourself."

"Thank you, Alfred." She took a deep breath and walked toward the lobby, all the while wondering what word she needed to say to get a ride out of here should things go terribly wrong.

Michele didn't ask the people at the front desk for directions. She simply followed the sound of piano music and laughter. The restaurant was beautiful. Lots of windows, tables with white cloths and candles. She searched the room and found...*him.*

Holy wow, he looked great in a tux. His broad shoulders nicely filled out the jacket. The thin black tie dipped inside behind the single button he still had buttoned. The perfectly tailored tux highlighted his thin waist and long legs. Her mouth watered.

Jeff was scanning the crowd, too. Looking for her? When his gaze met hers, she lifted her hand to wave. His mouth opened in what seemed like surprise. He rose to his feet and lifted his hand back at her. His lips formed one word. *Wow.*

Her breath caught in her chest, her heart pounded, her lips turned up of their own accord. All the other people in the room, including the pianist, disappeared. There was only Jeffrey and that smile on his lips.

It was just like the first time she'd seen him. The way he looked at her heated up her insides.

Respectable business dinner, she reminded herself, even as she wondered what his kiss would taste like.

Twelve

At first, Jeff wondered if he'd been stood up. He suspected people were all asking themselves the same question he was asking: Where was his date?

The better question: Who was his date?

Dinner was about to be served and he was running out of small talk to use with the people at his table. He was disappointed by the lack of intelligent conversation and frustrated with the power plays. The organizers of the event had snubbed him and put him at a table with low-level hotel management—the flunkies. The big guys, the movers and shakers in the hotel industry, were all sitting together at the front of the restaurant next to the windows with the ocean views. They drank and laughed loudly, while he was at the back with these jokers, clenching his fists under the table. If his date didn't show up soon, he'd leave.

And then he saw her.

Michele walked into the room wearing an amazing pink dress that bared her shoulders and accentuated her breasts, waist and hips. Her blond hair was swept up into an intricate twist, exposing her sleek, long neck. One gold chain, with what looked like a heart, dipped into her cleavage. His gaze followed that heart and then traveled slowly back up to her parted glossy lips and smoky eyes. Lots of kissable skin.

"Wow."

She'd come to be by his side during a boring business dinner. That was all. But he was aroused just by looking at her. His heart pounded out a distress signal, a warning not to get in too deep. And then she raised her hand and smiled and things suddenly got real.

Someone at his table asked him a question, but he ignored it. His aching body was drawn to her and he was striding in that direction before he realized he'd risen from his chair.

"God, you look gorgeous." He took her arm without even thinking about it.

"So do you." Her cheeks pinked and she looked at him from under her long lashes. Her voice was husky, and soft enough that only he heard her. No flirtatious tone. She said those words like she meant them.

Hell, he was going to have to sit down.

Guiding her to his table, he wished they could leave now and go somewhere quiet to be alone, but the food was arriving and she'd come all this way for him. To help him represent his dream to the industry movers and shakers. He needed to at least feed her before he whisked her away.

He pulled her chair out and she kept her gaze on his. "Thank you."

Sexy without trying. He was in big trouble.

He sat quickly and introductions were made around the table. Michele smiled and shook hands with each person and offered appropriate comments as she did so. Like she was really listening.

"I ordered steak for both me and my date. I didn't like the other option." When he scooted his chair in, his thigh bumped hers under the table. The sudden touch was electric. She didn't move away, so he kept his leg right where it was.

"Ah, so you were going to eat mine, too." She smiled. "I might share if you're good."

Michele looked at him for a beat too long and then, as if she had to collect herself, she turned back to the lady next to her. "Tell me about your hotel. Does it have a restaurant?"

The food arrived and Jeff silently chewed his steak, watching Michele. Her whole body seemed to absorb what each person had to say. She laughed easily and gave restaurant advice. Calling each person by their first names, she seemed to remember what each one had told her about themselves. She interacted with them as if she was the one here to represent Harper Industries, not him, and she even added a few plugs for Casa Larga, as if she really cared about the place. The way she described the grounds and the private beach made *him* want to vacation there.

Hell, she was amazing.

Michele, in her gracious, easy way made him realize a cold hard truth—he was being a superior, egotistical ass. Like Finn.

And RW.

The thought that he was turning into his father made Jeff shift uncomfortably in his chair. He'd sworn to himself that he would never be arrogant, unfeeling and cruel like his father. He'd fought hard against those family genes for most of his life. That's why he'd created *Secrets and Sheets* in the first place—to stand up to the arrogant bastards who thought they owned the world. Sure, Jeff was cocky and funny on television, but he wasn't a superior jerk.

Was he?

Music started up outside and people left their tables and went out on the patio to dance.

She leaned over and whispered in his ear, sending chills bumps into his scalp. "Are you okay? You haven't said a full sentence in over an hour."

He scooted even closer and whispered back, "I'm an idiot."

They were eye-to-eye, breath-to-breath. She blinked and he could see confusion in her expression. "Did I do something wrong?"

"No, sweetheart. You're doing everything right."

She studied his expression.

"I swear, it's not you. I'm just…off tonight," he said.

"You're allowed. I don't expect you to be perfect."

Damn. She'd done it again.

Michele had a remarkable talent for surprising the hell out of him. Most people he knew did expect him to be perfect—his agent, producer, fans, dates and RW. As a kid, he was never good enough. For the show, Jeff was supposed to be at the top of his game and improving his performance every episode.

Before this moment with Michele, he hadn't realized how exhausting his life was.

"It happens to the best of us," Michele went on. "If this party isn't working for you, we could leave now, or…" She cocked her head toward the music. "We could shake out the sillies on the dance floor. That's what my sister does when she's feeling…off."

He lifted an eyebrow. He'd never heard that expression before. "Oh, it might be a lot sillier than you think. I don't know if you've heard the rumors, but the truth is, only one of the Harper men knows how to dance and it isn't me. Sure you want that kind of embarrassment?"

"No worries. My standards are really low. The first and last time I danced was at my junior prom. And I'm not sure you could call that dancing."

He stood to pull her chair out and whispered in her ear, "A dancing virgin, then."

Her lips quirked. "I guess so."

When she rose, she gave his arm a squeeze, sending off an alarm that reverberated low and deep in his psyche. "I didn't have time to mention it before, but I want to thank you for paying my sister's fees. I will pay you back. I promise."

"That's not necessary."

"I think it is. But I am grateful for the gesture." She kissed his cheek. "Dance with me."

She turned to walk outside, expecting him to be right behind her. He wasn't.

Suddenly, he regretted agreeing to dance. What if he couldn't hold her, touch her, feel her velvety skin on his, without wanting more?

Without wanting too much.

He exhaled slowly through his nose and stiffly followed her outside.

"Over here," she called to him. "I thought I lost you. Isn't this place beautiful? The Monterey pine grove and the moonlight shining on the water?"

He couldn't talk. All he could do was feel.

He wanted this, needed her.

The music slowed at that moment and he took Michele in his arms and held her close.

He didn't want to let her go. He had to keep reminding himself that this was business, not a date, not the start of something he couldn't finish. A woman like Michele would want more than he could give her. She deserved more than him.

Michele put her head on his chest and he pressed the small of her back, holding her against him. She felt good in his arms, really good.

"How do my moves compare to those at the junior prom?" he asked, his voice sounding surprisingly normal.

Gazing up at him, she smiled. Her dimples drove him crazy. "You, Jeffrey Harper, are so much better. This is definitely dancing."

Michele had one hand on his shoulder while the other was wrapped around his waist. As they swayed to the love song, he listened to her breathing, felt her heart beat against his chest.

Slowly, he ran a finger over her bare shoulder. Silky and soft. He wanted to kiss the curve of her there, the hollow, and work his way up to her delicate earlobe.

"Michele?"

"Hmm?"

"My closest friends call me Jeff."

Her breath caught. "Jeff," she said softly.

The sound of his name on her lips lit a fire in his groin. Feelings he had not felt in a long time burned through his blood.

He wanted this, to hold someone who was compassionate and real. He wanted to experience...something. Everything.

Was this what his siblings had meant by feeling a real connection?

"Remember when you kissed me in the kitchen?" he asked.

She stopped swaying and buried her face against his chest. "I don't know why...that was so...embarrassing."

"Yes. It was...for me." He tipped her chin up so he could see her eyes when he said, "I really messed it up. Will you please do it again?"

Her lips parted in surprise and then turned up into the sweetest smile he'd ever seen. "I promised myself I wouldn't kiss you again."

"Pretty please? What do I have to do, Miss Cox? Juggle clams and catch them in my teeth?"

She burst out laughing and then covered her mouth. She cut her eyes to see if she'd bothered anyone on the dance floor. He was sure she'd only bothered him.

Her laughter did amazing things to him.

"You got me," she said and smiled.

He liked the sound of that.

She put her hand on his cheek and rose up on her toes. This time, when her lips touched his, he kissed her back. Not gently.

It had been too long since he'd kissed a woman he cared about and his body reacted with a landslide of need, ache, fire. It felt good. Real.

He deepened the kiss, diving in, tasting, touching, wanting. He pressed her body to his. Enjoying the sensation of her breasts against his chest, her thighs touching his. He stroked her shoulder with his free hand. God, her skin was so soft, her lips perfect.

He'd come to this event to make a good impression on the other hotel owners and now he didn't give a damn about any of them. He kissed Michele as if he'd never kissed a woman before and still he wanted more.

He felt like he could never get enough.

The band played a faster song and he reluctantly pulled away to look at her. Her cheeks were flushed, her eyes hooded. Sexy. Her hips moved to the sensual beat. He liked it.

He liked her.

Putting his hands on her hips, he tried to follow along, not quite catching up. She raised her eyebrow and slowed the movement, rubbing against him as she did, pressing, teasing. Hell, he liked that more. Cupping her jaw, he kissed her again, soundly.

Out of the corner of his eye, he saw a woman dressed in a black sequined gown pass by, puffing on her cigarette. She turned around and took a long look at Jeff kissing Michele.

"You're disgusting," she snarled at Jeff. "First the maid in the hotel and now this? Stay away from him, honey. He's a pig." The woman threw her cigarette on the patio, ground it out with her heel and stomped away before either one of them could say a word.

Anger boiled inside him.

"Dammit!" How dare Finn's manipulations ruin this, too.

"Ignore her," Michele said softly. "She doesn't know

you. People only see what they want to, not what's true. You are so much more than a stupid GIF."

He turned his head and studied her. Was *she* for real? Could she see him—past the show, the press, the GIF?

Matt's words rushed back to him.

Show her who you are without the smoke and mirrors. No stage lighting. No props. Just two real people being...normal.

And suddenly he wanted normal. Wanted real.

More. He wanted real *with* Michele. The thought alone should have scared him. He should've pushed himself away because he knew he'd only hurt her in the end. But he was too caught up in the heat and her sparkle to do anything except pull her into his arms and kiss her like no one was looking. The little sound of contentment she made at the back of her throat went straight to his groin. He lifted his head to look at her. She still had her eyes closed and the sweetest smile on her face. This had nothing to do with the chef job—he'd have to figure that out later—it had everything to do with the sensations pulsing through him. He couldn't hold back the tidal wave of want that overtook him.

"Let's take this off the dance floor." His voice was little more than a growl.

Breathing heavily, she nodded.

"Tonight, the chef competition is on hold. Our date has nothing to do with that."

"I didn't believe it did."

"Good. I had activities with the other women, but nothing like a date. I wouldn't want you or anyone else to think this is how I operate."

"No. Of course not."

He led her down the torch-lit pathway, away from

the restaurant and patio dance floor and past the Monterey pine grove. He was on the hunt for a quiet alcove far away from the dinner party and prying eyes, any place to be alone with Michele and not have to think or be judged.

"What's that?" She pointed toward the redwood structure perched like a beacon high above the rugged Big Sur coast.

"A wedding pagoda. Couples come from all over to be married under that canopy."

"It's lovely. I can just imagine the bride and groom standing there, gazing into each other's eyes, with the waves rolling in, whispering sweet promises below."

"You're a romantic."

"And you're not?"

"Not about weddings, no. My parents blew that institution sky-high."

"Ah, so that article I read about you was true. You will never get married."

"Don't believe everything you read. I will get married, but it sure as hell won't be for love."

Her jaw dropped. "What would it be for? A business arrangement? The trading of camels? A joining of kingdoms?"

She was joking. He wasn't.

"Something like that. I wouldn't want my bride to fall in love with me. I'd just hurt her like my parents hurt each other."

"It doesn't have to be that way. My parents married for love and rarely argued. They raised me and my sister in a great home before they passed away. What if you fall in love with your bride and you both live happily ever after? It could happen."

"Not to me. I don't have the chemical makeup for it."

She blinked. "You can't fall in love?"

"No. And I won't hurt anyone because of my screwed-up DNA."

"I don't believe that."

"That's because you aren't like me. You're warm and caring. Sweet. I see you going for the wedding pagoda and the happily-ever-after, Michele. I hope it sticks for you. I'll take the no-drama, no-stress business contract in front of a judge. It's better that way."

"That seems so...unfeeling."

Yeah, that's what he was trying to tell her. No matter what was happening between them tonight, he didn't have any of those feelings. Never would.

He was cold.

"Let's find a fireplace," he said.

He didn't tell her that he'd already agreed to a loveless marriage when the restaurant was completed.

Why ruin the best date he'd had in years?

Michele sat beside Jeff on a couch in front of a rock fireplace. They were alone and far from the dinner party. An owl hooted in a tree nearby.

"Cold?" He took his tuxedo jacket off and wrapped it around her shoulders. Not with him sitting this close. Her body was still humming from his kisses.

She put her head on his shoulder and looked up at the stars. "So beautiful."

"Got that right." He was looking at her.

It surprised her. He'd dated so many gorgeous women, did he really think she was beautiful?

She laced her fingers with his. She really wanted to touch him. All over.

With her head still on his shoulder she whispered, "Can we just stay here forever?"

"What about the restaurant I have to finish? And the world-renowned recipes you're going to create?"

She sighed. What if she couldn't create any recipes anymore, world renowned or otherwise? She knew the answer. This would be her last night with Jeff unless she could find the magic.

"Well, if we have to go back to reality tomorrow—" she started.

"Let's make this a night to remember," he finished and punctuated the thought by cupping her jaw and kissing her lips.

He was such an amazing kisser. When he sucked on her bottom lip she moaned with delight. She turned her head so he could have better access. He gripped her hair and pinned her in place. His tongue thrust in and out. In and out. She imagined that tongue doing wicked things between her legs and she moaned again.

"Pull up your dress," he growled. "I want to touch you."

She hesitated. The man had just told her that he couldn't fall in love. He wasn't interested in a real marriage, only one that was advantageous to his business. He was a playboy who dated anyone he wanted. And he was right, she wasn't like that at all. She wanted to love, to feel everything, and to make a life and family with her soul mate, like her mother did.

But the expression on his face—dark, determined, needy—was her undoing. No one had ever looked at her like that before and she longed to feel sexy, just once. She stood and crinkled up the material from the hem of her dress until her legs were exposed.

"More," he said.

She swallowed and pulled her gown up further until he could see her pink panties. They matched the dress and probably looked almost nude in the light of the fire.

"Come here, sweetheart." He crooked his finger at her.

Her brain kept trying to tell her that Jeffrey Harper was the opposite of her soul mate. He was sexually experienced and hot enough to burn her to ash. He was a one-night guy and she didn't do one-night stands, and she didn't sleep around at work either. It wasn't in her chemical makeup to shut feelings off and walk away. And it certainly wasn't like her to hook up with a take-charge kind of a guy who had the power to hurt her professionally and personally. But part of her was drawn to the sadness in Jeff, the deep pain he tried to hide.

There was a heart in that wide, muscular chest. Jeffrey just didn't know it. Maybe if she could show him how to love…

She came toward him and he pulled her on top of his lap. She straddled his legs, the only thing between them were her panties and his tuxedo pants. He was so deliciously hard. He ran his hand up her leg starting at her calf and going higher, higher.

"Kiss me," she whispered.

"Oh, babe, your wish is my command."

He kissed her shoulder, her neck, along her jawline. When he finally made his way to her lips she met him with her tongue. He opened to her, letting her lick his lips, taste, explore. He sucked in a sharp breath and she knew she was doing something right.

One of his hands rubbed, petted, traveling up her legs, driving her wild. Their tongues danced. She'd never been kissed like that before. When he got to her glutes, he gave them a squeeze. Her heart pounded hard in her chest. The world was spinning around her. She gripped his shoulders to stabilize herself, enjoying this man and his incredible lips. His finger ran underneath the elastic of her panties. She stilled in his arms. Was he really going to—the thought was cut off when his hand was suddenly touching her inside her panties.

"Okay?" he asked.

She nodded. More than okay. She hadn't felt like this in years.

He petted her, making her wet.

A voice in her head tried to remind her that she was outside a party where anyone could walk by, anyone could see what he was doing to her. But what he was doing was far too good.

Her own moans blocked out any inner voices.

"You like that?" he asked.

"Oh, yes."

He kept petting. Kissing. Driving her wild.

His finger went inside. He tugged gently, hitting a sweet spot she didn't know she had.

"Oh. " Was all she could muster. He felt so good. Before she knew it, her hips were moving with his hand's movements. Her breath and heart beat racing.

"Come for me," he growled against her neck. "Let go."

The words, hoarse and encouraging, undid any reserve she'd been clinging to. She threw her head back and rode him up and over the abyss. Moaning as the feelings—raw, rich, delicious—rolled through her.

Just then, a flash went off.

"Thanks, Harper!" a man shouted and ran off.

She blinked in surprise.

Jeff cursed while quickly lifting her off his lap. "Head down," he said in a clipped sharp tone. He brought his jacket up to cover her face. But it was too late. A photographer had snapped a picture of them in a decidedly unrespectable dating moment. And…there was the fact that she'd oh-so willingly flown over the abyss with her potential boss. No one would know that they mutually agreed this date had nothing to do with the chef position.

She'd thrown gasoline on his already damaged reputation, setting fire to everything.

Jeff pounded his pockets, coming up empty. "Do you have a cell phone?"

She handed him hers.

"Alfred, come to the side lot and get Michele the hell out of here," Jeff barked into it.

Paparazzi *here*? In the middle of freaking nowhere? Why wouldn't those bastards leave him alone?

He glanced at Michele. She was pale and still had his jacket held up to her neck as if she wanted to disappear. Hell, she looked so…beautiful. He'd never seen anything more gorgeous than Michele letting go in his arms. He longed to pull her back, nuzzle against her neck and whisper how much he wanted to have her come again and show her how much he still wanted her. Damn the paparazzi! He'd lived with the press long enough to know that the one night would have consequences for both of them. Sweet Michele—a woman who was already fighting insecurities—was about to have her reputation destroyed, too.

Unless he did something.

"Stay here. When Alfred arrives, climb in the limo and lock the door. He'll get you home safely," he told her.

"What about you? Where are you going?" Her voice was small. Hell, he'd messed this up for her. He was pissed at himself for wanting her so much. He should have had better control, been stronger. But even now he wanted her and was nearly desperate to throw caution to the wind.

"I'll stay here as long as it takes to find that photographer and make him delete the photo. I'll get my own ride home. Don't worry, Michele. I'll handle it."

Her eyes widened. "How will you handle it?"

He wanted to beat it out of the guy, but he knew how these things worked. Jeff couldn't afford an assault and battery charge on top of everything else.

"The way Harpers do. With money." He spat those last words out. He really was becoming his father.

The limo pulled up. Alfred raced out of the car faster than Jeff had ever seen the old guy move and was quickly opening the door for her.

"Get her home safely," Jeff demanded.

"We can figure this out together. Please come with me." Michele reached out to him, but he stepped back.

"I can't." He was stepping back because he didn't want to hurt her. And he would, he was sure of that. A lady who wanted to get married for love would eventually hate him.

He couldn't love.

But his thoughts got messed up around her. He wanted to make love to her more than anything he'd ever wanted and wasn't sure why. He'd been with many women. Why was Michele different? Why did he need to touch her so badly? As if to prove the point, his hand was already on her shoulder before he could stop himself.

"Let Alfred take you back. This is my fault. I'm sorry."

Her crestfallen expression ripped a hole in his chest. "I'm not."

Damn. He wanted to kiss her so deeply that she'd never doubt how special she was. She made him want to be more than he could be. He wanted to feel. To be real. To fall in love. To love Michele deeply with everything he was not.

He exhaled slowly. "Don't misunderstand. I'm not sorry for our time together. That was…amazing. No, I'm sorry that I can't be a better man. You deserve more.

"Go. Now," Jeff finally managed.

"Jeff, please!" Michele called after him, but he didn't stop, wouldn't turn around.

He didn't understand why all the pieces he'd held together for so long were shattering like a bashed-in chandelier. Only one thing was crystal clear—he needed to protect Michele.

From himself.

Thirteen

Michele got up early to find Jeff. Had he come home at all?

She wanted to tell him that she wasn't mad at him. Concerned, confused, yes, but not angry. He'd given her the best night she'd had in a long time. She wanted to be with him again, in spite of everything, and she wanted to help him. If she could find him.

He wasn't anywhere in Casa Larga.

She wandered outside and found both Tonia and Freja sunbathing by the pool.

"Look who's here, Miss Sex Kitten," Tonia said.

"What?" Michele asked.

Freja pointed to the newspaper. "You made de front page."

Michele snatched up the paper. Sure enough, there she was on Jeff's lap with her dress hiked up to her thighs with the caption, "Who is Jeffrey Harper's New Sex Kitten?"

"Oh, no." Her heart sank. She sat on a lounge chair and read the scathing article. It painted him in a terrible light but the writer didn't know who she was.

"Good chefs win by their talents," Tonia snarled. "I can understand why you would try sleeping with the boss."

"A bad picture. Ees you, no?" Freja asked.

"Of course it's her. She wasn't here last night." Tonia gave Michele a withering look. "I demand you be disqualified from the competition. I guess Jeffrey won't do it, so I'm going to look for RW right now."

Tonia grabbed her cover-up and marched into the house.

Freja tsked. "Too bad. I like you better than that one, but she ees right. Ees best if you quit."

They were both right.

God. She'd messed things up. She really, really liked Jeff. A lot. And she'd let him down. The one night she was supposed to help improve his reputation, she gave in to her desires and let herself go on his lap. Even though it was one of the best dates of her life, she'd hurt his reputation even more. She'd been selfish and lost the job that would save both her and her sister while hurting the first guy she'd dated in a long time. Who does that? Feeling terrible, she decided she'd go clear the air with him, make sure he was okay, and then…she'd leave.

Angel was heading down the hallway in RW's private wing when she saw a woman opening doors and peeking inside each room.

Who was she? What was she looking for? And where was the guard?

Cautious, Angel stepped back inside RW's room and closed the door. The woman didn't seem to be dangerous. She was barefoot and wearing a pool cover-up, for Pete's sake, but Angel couldn't take any chances. Not with Cristina and her little boy hiding here from Cuchillo's gang. Angel had made many mistakes in her life, including trusting the wrong man and staying with him when she should have left. She wasn't that girl anymore. She was a woman who had escaped all of that. Now she had to protect everyone—RW's family and her own.

She called security. "A young woman is wandering the halls in RW's private wing. Please escort her back to wherever she is supposed to be. And make sure the guard is stationed at his post in the next thirty seconds, or RW will fire him."

Not even a minute later, Angel heard a commotion in the hall.

"*Idiota!* Get your hands off me," the young woman yelled. The voice sounded familiar. Was she one of the chefs? Had Angel made a mistake by calling security?

Angel was about to go and correct the situation when her phone rang in her hand. "*Hola?*"

"Oh, Angel. Good, I'm glad you answered." It was Chloe. "Can you come to Matt and Julia's house? Dad's here, too."

RW left Casa Larga and went to Julia's house? Something was wrong. With her heart in her throat she asked, "RW...is he...okay? Is Julia? What's going on?"

"It's about Jeff. Another picture has popped up in the newspaper this time. I'm worried this will convince Jeff that he can't have a real relationship and he'll marry for the wrong reasons. We need to figure out a way to convince Jeff that he is not like Mom and Dad. Please come here so we can talk. We need your help."

Jeff was on the restaurant work site, hammering nails with the rest of the framing crew.

He didn't want to think, or talk; he just wanted to pound nails. Over and over until his muscles screamed louder than his brain. He couldn't stop seeing the anguish on Michele's face after he'd forced her to walk away. After he'd given in to temptation and landed them both on the front page.

He hadn't been able to find the jerk who'd snuck up and interrupted the best thing Jeff had experienced in years. He still craved Michele more than anything. A cold shower, two cups of espresso and a terrible night's sleep hadn't dampened his desire for her. If anything, time had made his need for her grow, like an unquenchable thirst. The intensity of his desire for him scared him.

But that was too freaking bad because he couldn't have her, especially not now.

Everyone had seen the photo of Michele in his lap at the convention. They would assume he couldn't keep it in his pants. And they'd take Michele down with him. He was glad no one knew who she was and he planned to keep it that way. He wouldn't tarnish her career with his own smutty one.

This whole fiasco only proved his point about how different they were. This was why he couldn't marry someone who loved him or love them in return. No matter how good Michele felt in his arms, how amazing her lips tasted, he couldn't touch her again. He'd only ruin her.

He pounded nails as hard as he could.

By midday, Chloe showed up at the work site. She was about to duck under the chain when Jeff called to her, "You can't come in here without a helmet. Construction site rules."

"Then you come out!"

Hell, no. "Can't. Busy."

She gave him the stink eye. "Hey, can you throw me your helmet?" she asked a worker who was taking his lunch break.

"Sure, pretty lady. As long as you bring it back."

Plopping the helmet on her head, she swung her leg over the chain and stomped toward Jeff. "You aren't returning my calls. What's wrong with the new phone I bought for you?"

"I turned my phone off. Too many crazy women calling for a good time." He wasn't joking. He held a nail between his teeth while he hammered another one.

"Come on, Jeff. Stop, so we can talk about what happened. I feel terrible."

She looked terrible. Hell, he didn't mean to hurt her, too. He put the hammer and nails down. "It wasn't your fault." No, this whole thing started and ended with him.

She pulled him away from the other workers before saying, "I'm worried about you. You've got to stop thinking you can't connect with people. Feel. By that picture in the paper, it looks like you feel something with Michele."

He narrowed his eyes. "You don't know what you're talking about."

She put her hands on her hips just like she used to do

when she was a little girl. "That might be the official story, but I know it's bull. You did make a real connection with her. I can see it in your reaction."

He couldn't look her in the eye. "Everything is fine."

"Really? Then talk to Michele. The poor girl doesn't deserve to be ignored."

He looked down at his hands. They still ached to touch her. They still belonged to a man who could turn Michele's life into a media circus. "I can't be near her right now."

Chloe let out a deep breath. "Because you like her. A lot. And you're scared."

He didn't respond.

"So, what are you going to do about the chef competition? Those three women are waiting for your answer. Which one will you choose?"

He still had no idea. He knew which one he wanted, but was she the best one for the job? Everything was even more confused than before.

"I haven't decided."

"Fine," she huffed. "One more event. We could invite the townspeople from Pueblicito to view the plans and the building site. The chefs can prepare their finest hors d'oeuvres and we'll see which one comes out the best."

It wasn't a terrible idea. The sooner he decided who the chef would be, the faster the marketing team could start the promo machine and drum up interest.

The sooner Michele would be gone…or permanently a part of the dream he was creating. "Okay."

"This coming weekend Dad has something going on, and he'll want to be at the event. How about the weekend after that?"

"Yeah. If the chefs are okay with staying that long. I

suggest having Dad increase their bonus." Twelve days. He could throw himself into his work and not have to think about anything until then. Not even Michele's soft skin. The memory of her on his lap crept into his thoughts. Since he didn't have a nail, he pounded his thigh to obliterate the vision.

Chloe shielded her eyes from the sun and studied him. "You should talk to Angel, or…someone. I really think it would help."

"I'll keep that in mind." He rose to go back to work, but then turned around. "Check in on Michele. Make sure she's doing okay. I didn't mean for any of this to happen."

"Or you could talk to her yourself."

He walked away.

He'd find someone else to date tonight. Someone he couldn't hurt.

It was time to start looking for a bride.

Michele was coming to grips with the fact that Jeff was avoiding her. It hurt.

She thought they'd had something special, but apparently, she'd read the situation incorrectly. She'd only been a one-night fling for him. And it hadn't even been a full night.

Part of her had known that truth at the time and yet she'd climbed on his lap anyway, because his lips and touch had felt oh-so good. She'd allowed herself to believe she could heal a playboy's heart. She'd risked her dreams and responsibilities on that hope.

Playing with fire only seemed to make her burn for more sizzling kisses, more caresses, more Jeffrey Harper.

He was the opposite of what she should be focusing on—taking care of her sister, learning how to cook again, finding a man to love her, starting a family.

But what she felt for Jeffrey didn't matter. She needed to put her energy into the one thing that *did* matter—landing this job.

There was one final competition, a sort of winner-take-all. She'd been asked to prepare hors d'oeuvres for a large party to show off the restaurant project. She knew this was a big deal for Jeff and was determined to do her best.

Sitting in her room, Michele scoured the internet looking for good Italian recipes, not finding anything that grabbed her. Nothing was good enough for Jeff's special night.

Closing her eyes, she whispered, "Help me, Mom. I need a little magic."

A light breeze came in through her window, lifting her hair off her face. Suddenly, she smelled sage, and rosemary. Opening her eyes, she squealed.

She knew what she was going to make.

Michele spent most of the next week in the Harpers' kitchen. It wasn't easy cooking meals next to the two other chefs she was competing against. They kept bumping into each other and fighting over the utensils, stove and ovens. All three chefs were making practice foods, getting them right.

Michele noticed that Freja was making a seafood cioppino. "You might want to rethink that one. Jeff hates seafood."

Freja pulled her white-blond hair up in a beautiful twist. "How ees dis possible? He took me fishing, said he loved water. He even swims like a fishy."

"Don't listen to her," Tonia said. "She's just trying to get into your head."

"I don't lie," Michele said.

Tonia shrugged. "We all know how you cheat."

Michele shook her head. "Suit yourself. Make all the fish hors d'oeuvres you want."

Freja looked at her ingredients, bit her lip and then put the fish back in the refrigerator. "I make something else."

The day of the event finally arrived. Michele had practiced enough. It was as if Jeff had flipped a switch inside her. All that sensual energy he'd awakened had to be channeled somewhere and she poured it into her cooking. She sampled each of her hors d'oeuvres. They were fantastic.

She went upstairs to get ready. Would it be the last time she'd see Jeff? She was incredibly sad at the thought. But he'd moved on, apparently, and she should stop driving herself crazy and move on, too. They were two different people who wanted different things.

He'd said it by the wedding pagoda. *You aren't like me. You're warm and caring. Sweet. I see you going for the wedding pagoda and the happily-ever-after, Michele. I hope it sticks for you. I'll take the no-drama, no-stress business contract in front of a judge.*

Well, she hoped he was wrong. She wanted him to find happiness and love someday, too. Even if it was with someone else.

Michele showered, applied her makeup, dried her hair and put on her flowing black pants, pale blue halter blouse and matching strappy sandals. Jeff seemed to like her bare shoulders. And she liked when he kissed them.

Shut up, Michele! she yelled at herself. Jeff wasn't

going to kiss her anymore. And she shouldn't be wanting him to.

She was here to be a five-star chef. Period.

Downstairs, people had started to arrive. She hustled to the kitchen and found Freja and Tonia had plated up their trays and were outside feeding the guests already. Darn it! They'd left her the two smallest, least attractive trays. She hurried. The first tray was for the fried giant ravioli stuffed with Italian sausage, spinach, parmesan, mozzarella, cherry tomatoes and a mixture of fresh Italian spices. In the center of the tray she had a tomato-and-red-wine-based dipping sauce that was to die for.

On the second tray, she placed her crostini, made with her homemade Italian bread. She'd kneaded savory fragrant spices, some of which she'd purchased from Juanita's, into the dough and had toasted the slices perfectly. She'd spread a thin layer of olive oil and goat cheese on top of the toasted bread. Purple and black dry-cured olives with rosemary and orange zest came next. The crostini were gorgeous and reminded her of a midnight sky. They made her think of the stars she and Jeff had looked at together. Arugula topped the olives. Around the edges of the tray, she carefully placed delicious prosciutto-, mozzarella- and risotto-stuffed fritters.

Everything smelled good, looked good, and would taste great.

Her magic was back.

She was ready.

Angel sat on the couch in Cristina's bungalow and checked the watch RW had given her for her birthday. They were late. RW and his family had already gone downstairs for Jeff's restaurant unveiling. Angel's sisters were coming, too, but Julia and Matt had stayed home because Henry was sick. Angel thought about Jeff's predicament. Chloe, Matt and RW had all told her about Jeff's childhood. Jeff had refused to join what he called "an intervention" and claimed he didn't need their help.

From what the others told her, it was clear that Jeff did need some sort of help. Therapy was not a bad idea. Each of the Harper kids had their own crosses to bear because of the way RW and his ex-wife had raised them. The only role models Jeff had growing up were two adults who acted like they hated each other. Jeff had never known love and therefore thought he was incapable of giving love. But Angel knew differently. Hadn't RW proved that he was a loving man to her? Jeff could do the same. He just needed a gentle hand to guide him toward the feelings he was bottling up. Maybe Michele was the nice one he needed.

Angel glanced at her watch again. If Cristina didn't hurry, they would miss Jeff's big speech.

"Come on, Cristina. What's taking so long?" Angel's patience was growing thin. It was stressful having the woman and her child staying in Casa Larga. Protecting so many people kept Angel on edge.

Cristina walked out of the bedroom and closed the door behind her. "Sebastian doesn't want to go. Maybe I should stay here."

"No, you need to get out of this bungalow and have some fun. I'll get someone to watch Sebastian so you can take a break."

Angel instructed one of the maids to babysit. She knew Cristina needed more than just a break for one night. The young woman craved the same things Angel did—a free life with her family outside the gang. But Cristina and her son *could* go somewhere else and be happy and safe. Over time, Cuchillo would lose interest in wanting to make Cristina pay for deserting the gang. And since Cristina hadn't personally witnessed Cuchillo's sadistic crimes, not like Angel, she wouldn't be a strong witness for the prosecutor. Cuchillo wouldn't have to hunt Cristina down and seal her lips forever.

Angel wished she could be that lucky.

Fourteen

"Thank you all for coming." Jeff stood next to the newly framed restaurant, the sky peeking through the bare wood bones. He lifted his voice so everyone in the crowd could hear him while searching the faces for Michele.

Even though he knew he shouldn't.

He wanted to see her.

There had to be fifty people from Pueblicito there to take a look at the new building and taste the food from the competing chefs. *Shareholders*, Dad had called the townspeople. It appeared that RW Harper was going to donate a percentage of the hotel and restaurant profits to them after all. At least, Jeff hoped that was the case, otherwise his father had suckered him into lying to these people.

"As you can see, the restaurant is coming along

nicely. We expect to be open for business right on time." It was going up fast and even in its early stages, it looked amazing.

The crowd cheered.

Pride bloomed in his chest. This was what it felt like to be proud of his accomplishments. Damn, he'd missed this feeling. It surprised him that he was so thrilled with a project that involved the home he used to hate. Working with his father had been better than he ever dreamed possible.

"The plans for both the restaurant and the hotel are pinned up on the wall for you to review at your leisure, but let me set the mood first. Pretend you have just arrived in Plunder Cove, weary and hungry. You walk up those steps…" He pointed to a grassy hillside. The steps had yet to be made. "…and see this wood-sided building, both rustic and charming, with views out to the Pacific Ocean. The shape, the wood, makes you think of—"

"A pirate ship!" someone in the crowd interrupted.

He nodded and one of the old women in the crowd, called out, "Knew you'd do this right. We've got faith in you, Jeffrey."

He pressed his hands to his chest and made a tiny bow. Then he went on to describe his vision for the restaurant. Freja passed by him with a half-empty tray. Tonia was on the other side of the patio surrounded by a group of hungry people. "And please, eat up. We have three of the finest chefs in the world here with us tonight. Enjoy."

He scanned the crowd.

And then he saw her.

Standing off to the side holding her tray, Michele

was watching him. The look on her face resembled pride—in him. It made him want to grab her, press her up against the wall and kiss those pretty lips. Ignoring all the warnings going off in his brain, ignoring everything he'd told himself as he'd stayed away from her for days, he strode toward her, determined to pull her away and get a taste.

He'd drink until he was full and then he'd think about the reasons why he shouldn't have her.

A man bumped into him. "Water!" the guy choked.

Another person started coughing, and another. Someone behind him said, "We need flan, or milk. This stuff is too spicy!"

Jeff looked around. One guy had tears running down his face while his wife tried to console him. What was going on?

"I thought it would be sweet." A woman walked up to Michele and pointed. "My husband can't eat spicy peppers. He might have to go to the ER because of you!"

Michele blanched. "What?"

The three sisters from Pueblicito came to her aid. Nona said, "I love the sauce. Habaneros are my favorite."

"Me, too," Flora nodded.

"Just the right kick," Alana added.

"Habaneros?" Michele looked at Jeff, her face pale. "I didn't put peppers in the sauce."

"Are you sure?"

"No, I...don't think I did..." She bit her lip, indecisive. She tasted the sauce and her face went eyes widened. "There are peppers in this sauce."

Jeff ran his hand through his hair. Every molecule in his body, especially those below his waistline, screamed at him to ignore the mistake and give her a chance. Let her stay. No, make her stay. But would he let Tonia or Freja continue in the competition if they messed up as badly as Michele had with the sauce when it wasn't her first mistake? Maybe not.

Deep down he knew he wanted to forgive any mistakes Michele made because he wanted her. He couldn't be objective about Michele. With her he was in a constant state of need. He shouldn't feel needy when he was supposed to be in control. She was ruining him in more ways than one. His gut burned as if he'd swallowed a whole habanero chili.

He had to grow up, be the boss he was supposed to be and let her go. He turned to the serving staff and asked them to bring water and milk right away.

"Michele, I don't know what in the hell happened, but this is unacceptable. You know how important this night is for me," he said. "I need a chef who is consistent." Disappointment and sadness gripped him. He had to cut her out of the competition, which meant he might never see her again.

"I know, Jeff. I'm sorry. This won't reflect on you. It's not your fault, it's my responsibility. I'll clean it up before I go." The sparkle he loved so much was gone. She raised her voice. "Ladies and gentlemen, I apologize that the sauce was too spicy. Anytime there is a mistake in the kitchen a good chef always makes it right. Please do not leave yet. I will create something special for you to cool your tongues."

Before she ran back to the kitchen her gaze met his. "I'm sorry."

The three sisters from Pueblicito cornered Jeff.

"You were too hard on her." Nona eyed him ferociously.

"Yeah, she's a nice lady who makes great food," Alana agreed. "Did you try those giant ravioli? I'm gonna be dreaming about them for weeks."

"I like the ball things and the olives. Michele was my favorite. Those other two chefs?" Flora shook her head. "Not even close."

"I can't have a chef who makes mistakes like that," he said to them. "It's business."

"I see. You never made any mistakes." Nona's expression was all too knowing. As if she'd witnessed some of the hell he'd lived through. "No one ever counted you out? Treated you like you were dirt and then kicked you to the curb?"

His jaw dropped. How did she know all of that?

"Nona's right. Give her another chance," Flora said. "She's the one for you."

Alana smacked her lips. "You think she has any more of those ravioli in the kitchen?"

The old women were right. Michele's food tonight was sparking with magic. She was consistent with every dish except the dipping sauce.

Why had she messed it up? It didn't make sense.

Michele was beside herself. What had happened? She hadn't used habanero chilis since the night she made the grilled cheese sandwich for Jeff. Someone had put those peppers in her dish.

She quickly rushed to make a specialty that the crowd would love. The only secret ingredients in the dessert would be the love and grief she was feeling right now. The passion for cooking had come back to her because Jeff had brought the magic back into her life. She was full of gratitude for that fact alone. But it was more than that. She was falling for him, hard. She knew he didn't think he could give her what she needed, but part of her wanted him anyway. Okay, most of her wanted him anyway. Even if she couldn't have him. And now she wouldn't have the job she needed, either. Jeff was sending her home.

She blinked back tears. How had things gotten so messed up?

At least the dessert was delicious. She tasted it to make sure and decided it was time to bring the guests in. The only number at Casa Larga that Michele had in her cell phone was to the Batcave.

Alfred, will you please tell Jeff to send the guests to the great hall?

Sure, Miss. I'll send up the Bat Signal.

The group came into the hall, filling it quickly. She was relieved that they'd all stayed because she was scared she'd ruined things for Jeff. She'd been so proud of him as he talked about his project. It was clear he was meant to create hotels, just as she'd been meant to create great food. Even if she'd lost track of herself along the way.

Michele stood behind the long table and encouraged the crowd to come forward to take a bowl. "This dessert is called 'zabaglione.' It is an Italian custard with some of my own special spices and marsala wine. Don't worry, nothing hot in this, just sweet and—"

"*Delicioso*," a woman said after taking her first bite. "This is amazing."

People started talking at once.

"Oh, my."

"This is the best thing I've ever tasted!"

"Fantastic. You've got to try this."

The rave reviews continued until someone in the crowd clapped and soon the room erupted in applause. They loved her dessert. Her heart melted. She'd made something everyone loved.

"Hey." Jeff stepped up to the table. "Can I talk to you?"

Her eyes welled. She blinked quickly, determined to keep things professional even as she walked out the door. She'd gone from needing this job financially, to wanting to help Jeff succeed in his grand and wonderful adventure. And now all of it was over.

"Of course. Take a bowl of zabaglione, too."

He took a bite. The look that spread across his face was mesmerizing. It was like a wave of happiness and joy. She wished he always looked like that.

What she didn't see? Shock. It was as if he'd known she could cook like this and had just been waiting for her to figure it out.

"Tastes like light, creamy heaven. Simply poetic. Welcome back."

She blushed with delight. "Thank you."

He took her hand. "Come with me."

It seemed like they were leaving the great hall. Was this it? Jeff was escorting her off the property?

They passed Tonia eating a bowlful of zabaglione in the corner. Her pretty face twisted with white-hot anger.

"Wait for me," he said to Michele. "I need to talk to Tonia."

Oh. Michele understood what this meant—Tonia had won the chef's competition. Michele was heartbroken. She wanted Jeff to have the best chef but something about Tonia made her feel like she had to watch her back. She'd lost the chance to be Jeff's chef. It was over. Did this mean she would never see him again? Never touch him. Listen to his deep voice, his laughter. Kiss his beautiful lips.

Walking over to Tonia, she heard Jeff say, "You don't like the zabaglione?"

"Not one bit. Why did Miss Nicey-Nice get a do-over?" Tonia spoke loudly to ensure that Michele heard her.

He crossed his arms. "My competition, my rules."

She scowled. "I didn't mess up my hors d'oeuvres, and yet I didn't get to make a dessert. She gets special treatment, has since night one. That's not fair."

"You mean fair like when you lied to me about being able to ride horses? It was clear you'd never been on a horse and yet you told me you rode them on your grandfather's ranch every summer." His tone was loaded with sarcasm.

"That was different. I explained it had been a while. I was rusty. I thought you understood."

"About the horses, yes. Not the habaneros."

Tonia put her hands on her hips. "Excuse me?"

"How did you know to use those specific peppers to sabotage Michele's dish?"

Michele could see the hardening around Tonia's eyes. She was furious. "What are you implying?"

"I don't imply. I state. You spied on us 'night one'

when I had Michele make the grilled cheese sandwiches."

Tonia blustered. "That's ridiculous. It wasn't me."

"Another lie. The cameras caught you on tape. I wanted to give you the benefit of the doubt for I, of all people, know how that feels, but it sure seemed like you were spying on us. Whatever the case, you did see Michele use those peppers and you'd know that I'd remember, too. It was easy to frame her that way."

Michele stood beside Jeff, facing Tonia. "You did it? Why?"

Tonia's dark eyes flared with anger. "Why do you think, Sex Kitten? You clouded his vision, made it so that no one else had a chance to win."

Jeff faced Michele. "She's right. You do cloud my vision so that I can't see anyone but you. You're my choice, Michele. Please, stay."

Angel and Cristina were on their way to the building site when RW texted.

Come to the great hall.

Okay. We'll be right there.

"I guess the party was moved inside," Angel said to Cristina. They were just about to enter the hall when Cristina grabbed her arm and pulled her back into the corridor.

"Oh, my God. Antonia is here," Cristina whispered.

"What? No, that's impossible." Poor Cristina was so frightened that she was seeing gang members everywhere she looked.

"Look over there. The woman with the dark hair in the corner talking to that tall redheaded guy. That's her. I can see the *cuchillo* mark on her from here."

Angel leaned over carefully and peeked. It was the same young woman Angel had seen snooping around in RW's wing. She'd thought she recognized her voice. And sure enough, the woman had a knife tattoo behind her ear. She gripped Cristina's shoulder as if her ex-boyfriend's blade had stopped her own heart.

"What do we do?" Cristina asked.

There was no question, Angel had to protect the ones she loved. Where was RW? Taking out her cell phone with trembling hands, she texted him.

The woman talking to Jeff is Cuchillo's sister!

Jeff was furious. How dare Tonia sabotage Michele.

"We're done here. Tonia, pack your things and—" Jeff began.

"Don't move!" a guard said, his gun drawn and pointed at Tonia. Two more guards joined him. Several people in the crowd cried out in fear and everyone scattered behind him.

"What are you doing? This is unnecessary," Jeff said. "Put your guns away."

Seeing guards and guns, Tonia lunged and grabbed Michele. Before Jeff had blinked, Tonia had a knife to Michele's throat.

"Get back," Tonia yelled. "All of you."

Michele's eyes were wide and pinned to him. The fear in them slashed him.

"Everyone, calm down!" Jeff lifted his hands and

willed Tonia to look at him. "Let Michele go and you can walk out of here. No one will stop you."

"Sorry, son, but she can't leave." Suddenly, Dad was beside him, whispering so that only Jeff could hear, "She's one of Cuchillo's gang members. She'll kill Angel."

Jeff stopped breathing. His Michele was in the arms of a killer.

"I walk out of here now. Understand me?" Tonia snarled. Her blade looked deadly.

Jeff's heart hit the floor. "Don't hurt her!"

To Tonia, RW said in an incredibly controlled voice, "We don't even know why you're here. Why pull this elaborate charade in my home?"

"I told you in my application video. Family is everything. Something was stolen from my brother a long time ago. He wants it back."

"I know you're looking for Angel. She's not here," RW said.

Tonia's gaze swung from Jeffrey's to RW's and back again. "Liar. Your PI said you're hiding her."

Jeff swallowed hard. RW's private investigator had been killed by the gang. Had they made him talk?

"Angel's here. I can feel it. Since she liked horses, we thought she might be working in your stables. The chef interview was the opportunity to snoop around. Plus, I wanted to win."

"Get the hell out of my home!" RW roared. "Tell your brother to leave my family alone or I will come for *him*. Got that, Antonia? Cuchillo has never met a man like me. I'll send that bastard straight to hell."

Tonia's eyes widened at the threat. She released

Michele and ran out the door. Michele slumped to her knees.

"I've got you, sweetheart." Jeff scooped her up and carried her to the couch. She'd been nicked. "Get me a clean cloth!" he yelled to the crowd. "Someone call the doctor."

RW sent one of the guards to follow Tonia and find the rock Cuchillo was living under. Cuchillo's gang had a knack for slipping off the grid and RW had lost the trail when they murdered his private investigator.

"Where's Angel?" one of the sisters said.

"Oh, Jeff. Did I ruin your night?" Michele's voice was so soft.

"No, sweetheart. You did everything right." Jeff held the cloth to Michele's cut and applied pressure. His heart was pounding so hard he thought it might explode. After a few minutes he checked the cut and was relieved to see it wasn't bleeding badly. "You're going to be okay, sweetheart." He wanted to carry her out of there and straight to his bed. He'd been so afraid for her and now he just wanted to touch her everywhere. Taste her. Feel her heart beating strongly against his bare chest.

"I was so scared," Michele said softly. She reached up and put her hand on his cheek.

"I know. Me, too." He ran the pad of his thumb along her cheek. He kissed her then, deeply, filling up all the dark wounds in his thundering heart, and let the world fall away.

Fifteen

Jeff had canceled his date for last night. No great loss. He hadn't been too excited about it anyway.

Right now, he was concerned about keeping Michele safe. He could have lost her and that thought alone terrified him.

After the doctor had checked her out and determined the flesh wound didn't need stitches, Michele said goodnight and Jeff walked her to her room. He wanted her in his bed but didn't say so because she seemed exhausted. He bunked down in the room next to hers in case she had nightmares or needed anything. He didn't sleep a wink because he was replaying the whole evening, trying to figure out what he would have done differently. He wasn't impressed with his performance but Michele had been strong, courageous and thoughtful from the start of the catered event to the dramatic end.

Her food, other than the sabotaged dipping sauce, was artistic and delicious.

Chloe had been right—the best chef had risen to the top. There was no doubt in his mind that Michele Cox was the chef for him. She'd proved that she was ready for the job and had bravely conquered her insecurities.

Jeff, on the other hand, was even more worried because the closer he got to Michele, the more he realized he was the wrong man for her. Hell, he and his screwed-up family had almost gotten her killed! He wouldn't have forgiven himself if Tonia had hurt her badly. He cared about Michele, wanted her, needed her more than he dared admit, but she couldn't fall in love with him. He wouldn't let her. It would kill him to hurt her like his father and mother had hurt one another. He wouldn't allow that to happen. He would have to get married to someone else.

When he heard her rustling around in her room, he knocked on the door.

Her expression was a mixture of happiness and surprise. "Jeff! Good morning."

He leaned against the door frame and breathed in her freshly showered scent. "Are you feeling okay?"

She touched the small Band-Aid on her neck. "Yes. I'm fine. It was just a scratch."

He breathed a sigh of relief. "Good. I've got plans for you. Thought we'd better get an early start."

Her brow creased. "Am I cooking or are we going on another outing?"

"Neither. You deserve a break. Plus, it has come to my attention that you've never been on a yacht before. And, as far as I can tell, you have not spent the day on the Harpers' private beach up the coast."

Her smile was so damned beautiful. "I can't say I have done either of those things, no."

He shook his head. "We'll have to rectify the situation immediately. Wear something warm for the morning and pack your bathing suit and a towel. I'll provide the picnic lunch. We need to celebrate your new job, Chef Cox."

Her mouth opened. "You really meant it last night?"

"Of course. I mean it this morning, too. I choose you, Michele. You're my chef."

She squealed and threw her arms around his neck. He stumbled backward, emotion warring inside him. Finally, he wrapped his arms around her and hung on. He kissed her right there in the hallway with her feet off the ground.

It seemed as if he couldn't stop kissing Michele Cox. His new chef. The woman he wanted but couldn't marry. What in the hell was he going to do?

His yacht was amazing. So much rich, dark wood and shiny metal. It looked like it was brand-new. It was the biggest boat she'd ever seen and she was surprised when he called it "the small one." Apparently, RW had several yachts all over the world. She couldn't fathom it. But she did love being on the gorgeous vessel and was lulled by the movement and the peaceful sea.

They'd been cruising up the coastline for twenty minutes already, close enough to shore so she could see the jagged edge of the bluffs and the coves. She wished they could keep going to San Francisco, or Hawaii, until she remembered she had a job to do in Plunder Cove. She didn't have to dream of running away anymore. She'd be living in paradise and working in the career she loved again.

She'd figure out a way to bring Cari to Plunder Cove, too. Surely, there was a group home nearby who could take her. It would take Cari a while to readjust to the new place but Michele was sure her sister would love digging her toes into the sand and meeting the horses the Harpers owned.

And getting to sail on the blue Pacific with Mr. Sexy was a nice perk. She understood why he had pushed her away for a week. He was busy with the restaurant, and the competition had been difficult. Plus, he was distancing himself because they were two people who wanted different things. She agreed it was best they didn't spend too much time together because her silly heart always wanted more. She kept reminding herself that Jeff didn't want to, or was unable to, give her more of himself. She needed to be realistic. This connection they had wasn't going to last.

"Want to drive?" he asked.

"Can I?" She felt like a kid being handed the car keys for the first time.

"Come on over." He stepped back and made room for her. Tentatively, she put her hands on the wheel.

"Relax. It's easy." His deep voice rumbled in her ear, sending delicious shivers up into her scalp. And then he put his hands on her shoulders.

Relax? Her body heated up and her thoughts zeroed in on the way his large hands felt on her. Why had she worn a sweatshirt? She wanted his hands on her skin. He pressed into her and she could feel his hard stomach muscles against her back. How she wanted him. She closed her eyes and breathed in his scent. Her eyes flew open again when she remembered she was driving his expensive boat.

Besides, she had no business enjoying his hands on her body or daydreaming about his lips. She was going to be working for him and didn't have any idea what impact their new working relationship would have on their…situation. She didn't really know what to call their relationship.

They had smoking hot chemistry but that was the *easy* part. The dangerous part. When she was close to him she wanted to climb into his lap, let herself go, and take him with her to ecstasy. It was going to be hard enough working for him and wanting to kiss him every day, but she couldn't *relax* and let down her guard or she'd fall hard for him. She was already tilting heavily in that direction with her feet slipping. One more of his sizzling, mind-melting kisses might topple her defenses.

Giving in to her desire for him again could only end badly for her. He'd made it clear that he wouldn't fall for her. She'd be a fool not to believe his warning. No matter how many times she fantasized about Jeff Harper, he wasn't her dream man. He'd eventually marry someone else and she…she'd have to let him go. Which was going to be incredibly difficult now that she would be working for him.

Jeff directed her to pull into an alcove. He dropped anchor and turned off the engine.

He stripped off his sweatshirt and for the first time she got to gaze at his lean, hard chest, arms and stomach in person. The pictures in magazines didn't do justice to his amazing physique. Her fingers itched to touch the red curls on his chest and trace each muscle all the way down the dark V into his shorts.

"Ready?" he asked.

Nope. Her defenses were crumbling. She was in serious trouble here.

He rowed the dinghy to the shore and she helped him pull it up on the sand. It was a pretty little beach with white sand and clumps of rocks at the water's edge.

He tossed his bangs out of his eyes and grinned like a kid. "I haven't been here in years. The old firepit is still there. And the inner tube Matt and I used to float around on. This is like a blast from the past. Let's see if we can catch a crab in the tide pools."

"Okay. Let me just put this blanket down and I'll catch up."

He gave her a thumbs-up and jogged to an outcropping of rocks. She smiled as she stretched the blanket on the warm sand. She liked seeing him like this. Boyish, not so intense.

She needed to watch herself.

She had no business playing with fire.

But she really, really wanted to. Once again, she had the desire to show him what love looked like. If only he could see how easy it was to let himself go, to allow himself to feel, then maybe he could open his heart to her. She believed a loveless man could learn to love. She wanted to give that gift to him.

And today—with the chef job lined up and her sister taken care of—she felt brave.

So when he jogged back and sat beside her she said, "Is this a real date?"

He ran a finger down her shoulder. "As real as it gets."

He hadn't seen anything yet. "I seem to recall our

last date was rudely interrupted. Can we pick up where we left off?"

He grinned. "You want to sit on my lap?"

"Yes. But, no. I have another idea." The last time she climbed on his lap things flew out of her control too quickly. If she was going to show him how to feel loved she would need to slow things down a bit.

"Lie back on the blanket."

His gaze was intense—curious and cautious—but he did as she asked.

"Now put the towel under your head. I want you to watch me touching you."

She didn't know what she was doing, and it was probably a really bad mistake, still every inch of her begged to get close to him.

He tucked a towel under his head and watched her.

Starting at his fingertips, she made slow, sensual circles around the nail beds and gently petted his knuckles. She traced each bone and vein she could see under the skin.

He had a fine sprinkle of freckles across the back of his hand. She rubbed his skin softly, slowly, feeling the hairs on his hand lift with her touch.

He had large, strong hands. Turning them palm up, she traced every line. She looked at him, silently asking permission to keep going.

"It feels good." His voice was rough.

She was feeling things, too. Lots of heat. Tons of want. She'd never touched anyone like this before, never wanted to. She couldn't seem to get enough.

She massaged his fingers, pressing deep into the pads of his thumbs. He curled his fingers around hers, giving her hand a squeeze, like a hug.

"Your arms now." Why was she whispering? They were alone on a private beach.

She circled his wrist bones, dragged her nails up his forearm and then softly rubbed her way back down toward his wrists. Goose bumps rose on his arms. She pressed harder and smoothed them back down. Squeezing his biceps, she marveled at the muscles beneath her hands. Turning his arm over, she used her nails and soft touch along the length of the underside of his arm. His skin was smooth, not freckled on this side, silky. The bend of his arm was a kissable spot and she put her mouth there, pausing.

"Don't stop. Keep going." The growl in his voice made her look up. His gaze was intense.

She felt an answering zing in her core.

"Shoulders." Her voice was huskier than normal. She squeezed, massaged and ran a feather touch over his shoulder muscles.

God, he was so beautiful.

She ran her palm over his collarbone and dipped her fingertip into the hollow of his neck. She could feel his pulse beating fast there. He was breathing faster now, too, as was she. This slow, burning touch was working her up quickly.

Honestly, she'd been burning since that incomplete night on the coast. Maybe longer.

She caressed his neck. She ran the back of her fingers over his strong square jaw and chin.

She didn't want to miss one inch of him.

His eyes watched her every move. That sexy look was giving her goose bumps of her own. She wanted him. Inside her. She'd never felt such a desperate heat before her.

His lips twitched as if he knew what this was doing to her. If he gave her his signature cocky grin it was game over.

She cleared her throat and pressed her legs together against the ache building there and placed both her palms on his pecs. She made circles over the muscles and played with the nipple.

"Michele." Her name came out as a sexy growl that turned the heat to full melt-level. "Don't stop."

She rubbed the nipple again and twisted his chest curls. "I love your red hair."

"There's more to play with."

She lifted her eyebrow and looked down. *Oh*. He was fully aroused.

She was losing control of herself.

Very slowly, she caressed each stomach muscle of his gorgeous six-pack, working her way down. His breathing was fast now, almost as fast as hers. She circled his belly button with her middle finger and gently tugged on the hairs below it. Those were fun to play with, too, but she wanted more. Lifting her head, she saw heat and desire in his expression.

Good, she wasn't alone.

She ran her hand over his shorts, pressing against his erection.

He sucked in a sharp breath.

"Jeff?" she said quietly. "I want to kiss you."

The groan he made was music to her ears. He reached for her. Running his hand through her hair, he made a loose ponytail and gave it a gentle tug so that her chin tipped up.

She was looking into his eyes when he said, "Oh, babe. I want you."

It was as if she'd waited her whole life to hear those words. She pulled his shorts down and took him in her mouth.

This she needed.

Michele was touching him in a way he'd never experienced before.

With reverence.

With smoking heat.

Like she adored each millimeter of his skin and couldn't get enough of him. It was driving him wild. He was hard and wouldn't be able to hold on much longer. All this from her touch? Hell, what would it be like if he was deep inside all that heat? He needed to make love to this woman right now.

When she put her lips around his erection and sucked, a light show went off behind his eyeballs.

"Michele, stop," he somehow managed to say.

She pulled back, quickly.

"I'm too close. And I want to be inside you."

"Oh," she said softly.

He sat up and slid the bathing suit straps off her shoulders. He nuzzled the hollow of her neck and her moan almost made him lose it. "Sorry, sweetheart. This is going to be faster than I'd like but I want you too badly to wait. Take your suit off and I'll get the condom."

Thank God he'd decided to bring one.

She nodded. Her eyes were hooded with desire.

They were both ready. She was on her knees on the towel and beautifully naked.

"Hell, you are so damned gorgeous," he said and pulled her on top of him.

Skin-to-skin, her breasts to his chest, thighs pressed together, hearts beating hard, and he had one thought—*she's perfect*.

When she eased him inside and all that slick heat encased him, he closed his eyes to memorize her touch, everywhere.

And then she started moving and all thoughts left his brain.

She gripped his shoulders and her pace was fast. Apparently, she was close, too. He eagerly joined in the race to glory.

Cupping one of her beautiful breasts, he had the fleeting thought that he wished he could have spent time sucking and kissing her warm body.

Next time.

He sucked her nipple. She arched her back and cried out, coming quickly. He smiled and flipped her over so that he was on top. She wrapped her legs around him. Holding on to her thighs he went deep.

"Oh, yes, Jeff."

He kept going, loving the sexy smile on her face.

A few more thrusts and she cried out again, sending him over the edge. The light show going off behind his eyelids was better than Independence Day.

Michele and her gentle touch—her sparkle—was exactly what he'd needed. For the first time in a long time, he was free.

Sixteen

She didn't know how much time had passed, but she was hungry. Apparently, Jeff was, too.

"What do we have here?" she asked, rolling over to examine the picnic basket. "Did you make us lunch?"

He nodded. "Ham and cheese. My specialty."

"Can't wait to try it."

They sat side by side, legs touching, chewing in silence. Something had shifted between them, more than just giving in to sex. She could almost hear him thinking. But she didn't pry. Didn't ask the questions burning on her tongue.

He took his last bite, rolled the plastic wrap into a ball in his hand, and that's when the words poured out. "When I was six years old, I only ate mac and cheese."

"My sister was the same way! We had to trick her to try other foods."

"No tricks in my family, just demands. 'Eat your food, Jeffrey.'" He raised his voice to sound like a woman's. His mother's? "'Clean your plate or you won't get any food tomorrow.' That sort of thing."

"That's harsh."

"Sometimes I preferred to *not* eat. Like seafood night. Hell, I really hated squid."

She pressed her other hand to her heart. "I knew it. You didn't like my first dish! I wish I had made chicken."

He swallowed hard. "You didn't know. What happened to me when I was a kid wasn't reported in the gossip rags. Families don't talk about crap like this. They cover it in dirt and pretend it's dead."

She didn't dare interrupt.

"So yeah, back to the story. I was a picky kid and one night when I refused to eat, my mother said she'd had enough of my whining. Seafood pasta was her favorite dish and by God, her son was going to eat it without a peep. Dad wasn't there, but she made everyone else pretend that I wasn't there, either. After several minutes of being ignored, I threw my plate. Shrimp and noodles slid down the wall. I'd never seen my mother that angry before. She grabbed my arm and dragged me outside. I whimpered, but she said, 'Don't be a baby!' and pushed me inside the toolshed. 'Cry and I'm never letting you out.' And then she locked the door.

"Matt had told me to stay away from the shed because snakes crawled under the crack in the door. It was dark. The cold seeped in. I screamed until my voice was hoarse and my throat was raw. I tried to find a tool to dig out, but they were too high for me to reach. I dug in the dirt with my hands, but the ground was hard. It was freezing cold and I believed I was going to die in that shed all alone."

"Oh, Jeff!" Michele covered her mouth. She'd been psychologically beaten down by Alfieri, but she had been an adult at the time, one who could walk away from her abusive boss. Jeff had been a small child. She couldn't imagine what his mother had done to him deep down inside. She quivered with the need to touch him.

"When did she finally let you out?" Her voice cracked and her eyes burned with tears.

"Mother?" The chuckle he produced was sandpaper rough, humorless. "She didn't. She wanted to teach me not to be a crybaby. Emotions were a sign of weakness in her world. I understand now that something was broken in her genetic makeup that made it impossible for her to love anyone. She passed that broken gene to me."

A person incapable of loving? Michele still didn't believe it.

"I'm sorry, Jeff. No one should ever treat a child like that."

"You're crying." He gently wiped her cheek with the back of his hand.

Softly she said, "Emotions are human, normal. Especially for a little boy. Your mother should've known better. What did your father do when he found out?"

"Mother told him she'd ordered the staff to bring me in and they refused. It was a lie. Donna, the cook, heard me crying the next morning and found me curled up on the dirt floor of the shed. I'd wet myself from fear. When she opened that door, I ran to Donna and held on like I'd never held anyone. The staff banded together and told my mother that if she came into the kitchen, they'd all quit. Since my mother had no idea how to cook for herself, she agreed. I was safe from her in the kitchen." He tossed his hair off his forehead. "To this day, I don't like to eat alone or be in small dark places. That's why I don't usually take elevators."

She frowned. "But the GIF. You were in an elevator with a maid."

"Right. I was getting to that. The GIF was orchestrated by the hotel owner to ruin me." Absentmindedly, he stroked her hand. She hoped touching her calmed him as much as it did her. "Finn had threatened physical harm if we filmed his hotel. It was the first time a hotelier had been so aggressive. It made me wonder—what was the guy hiding? I took my own camera inside. Michele, I could bury Finn with the negative press on the kitchen alone. You would've been horrified."

"So, you got it all on film?" She watched his finger make lazy circles on the top of her hand and felt the touch all the way to her bones.

"And then some. Employees told me about bad workplace conditions. Safety violations. Codes ignored. Cover-ups and payouts. It was going to be the best episode ever." He let out a deep breath. "It'll never see the light of day because Finn stationed guards near the stairs, forcing me to take the elevator. I didn't have a choice. I had to get the tape to my producer. Stupid, rookie move. I should've expected Finn would pull some sort of devious stunt but this was…" He shook his head.

She was starting to understand. "Because you are uncomfortable in small places."

He laced his fingers with hers. "Yeah. I was already shaking when I got into the thing but there was a maid inside, so I tried to act cool. But when the elevator got stuck…" He shook his head. "It was one of my nightmares coming true."

She could feel his palm sweating and gave his hand a gentle squeeze.

"Then the maid removed her blouse."

"She *what*?"

"Yeah, that seemed strange, but women do weird things for celebrities. I was still pressing buttons to get the elevator going when the woman grabbed me and kissed me."

Michele's mouth dropped. "No! She was a total stranger!"

"It happened so fast. Nothing seemed real. When she started grinding against me, I woke the hell up. I tried to extricate myself. Gently. And then the lights went out. Blackness inside a box with only a slight crack of light under the door… It was like the shed. I was disoriented, terrified. When something grabbed my ass and pinched… I fought. The elevator lights came back on. The maid was on her butt, cussing up a storm. Her bra was torn. Her hair a mess. She had a red mark on her cheek."

The torment tangled in his starburst irises made her want to hug him, but she didn't move for fear he'd stop talking. She sensed he needed to get this out.

"Finn had tampered with the elevator, turned off the lights and paid the maid to come on to me while recording the whole thing. Releasing the first part, the sex scandal bit, ruined my career. He's holding the second part—the section that looks like I attacked the maid—as blackmail," he growled.

"She kissed and grabbed you! How can he use that against you?"

"Blackmail works best when the victim is caught on tape. People believe what they see, even a lie."

Shame heated her cheeks. Even she had believed Jeff was having sex in that elevator.

"This isn't fair! If a man had grabbed me in an elevator, I would've fought back, too, Jeff. Don't be ashamed. You did nothing wrong."

"Sweetheart, I'm six foot three and over two hundred pounds. Lots of muscle. She was tiny. You are tiny."

Something in his tone worried her. She cocked her head, trying to read his expression. Why did he mention her?

"I'd never hurt a woman, Michele, I swear." He looked at his hands as if he had weapons attached to his fingertips. "I have bad genes. I'm not good at relationships or connecting with people the right way. What if I am exactly like my mother?'"

Now she understood. "Oh, Jeff." She touched his face tenderly. "Have you talked to anyone about this? A doctor or therapist?"

"This is the first time I've told anyone this stuff. You don't understand. I'm trying to improve my reputation. If any of this gets out—my childhood, what really happened in that elevator—the Plunder Cove hotel will be done. I need to see this dream to the end. I need it to be the best it can be."

"It will be."

It had to be.

For both of them.

They didn't talk any more about his past—or his fears of what his future held—instead they had a nice day on the beach, exploring the tide pools, bodysurfing in the waves, walking on the sand. They held hands, kissed and talked. It had to be the best day she'd had in years.

They were making out like teenagers on the blanket when a speedboat pulled into the cove. Jeff started to sit up and Michele turned to look, too.

And saw a telephoto lens pointed at them.

"Get down," Jeff told Michele as he covered her head with his arms.

But it was too late.

The camera had caught him and a woman in a compromising position. Again.

Seventeen

They scrambled to grab their stuff and hop in the dinghy to make it to the yacht and catch up with the photographer. Jeff didn't care as much about his reputation as he did Michele's. Everyone already thought he was a playboy. Michele didn't deserve to have her name and personal details dragged through the dirt. If he could catch the guy, he'd talk some sense into him and pay whatever it took to kill the shot. "Hold on," he told Michele, glancing over his shoulder to make sure she was safe before he floored the yacht across the waves. He drove the boat like a madman for a few minutes before he acknowledged the truth.

It was too late. The cameraman had a speedboat and knew how to use it. Jeff slowed the vessel. Running he hand through his hair he faced her. "Sorry. There's no chance."

Her chin was high but he could see the worry in her eyes. "What will he do with the photos?"

"It'll be okay. Come here, sweetheart." He took her in his arms.

She lifted her head and the usual sparkle in her eyes had turned to flashing fear. "Those private pictures of us were...intimate."

Dammit. He saw all too clearly how he was messing up her life. "He'll sell them to the highest bidder. I'll get the PR team on it, see if we can buy them before someone else does."

"And if they can't buy them? What if Finn did this as another way to destroy you? He'll post them everywhere."

Yeah, he would. A firestorm raged inside his gut. How could he protect Michele?

"We have to stop Finn," she said with fierce determination.

He ran his finger down her cheek. "This is my fight, not yours. I shouldn't have dragged you into it. You shouldn't be with a guy like me."

She wrapped her arms around him and pressed her cheek to his bare chest. "What if I want to be with a guy like you?"

He sucked in a breath. Her words were a soft rain on the fire in his chest.

"Even with all my past?"

She rose up on her toes and pulled his lips toward hers. "Yes."

That night, Jeff slept alone. He'd kissed Michele goodnight and told her he had work to do. He'd worked with the PR team until dawn to no avail. They couldn't find any information on the photographer in the speedboat.

He'd never really worried about the women in his paparazzi shots before. This time he did care and would do anything he could to keep her out of his press.

What was he going to do about Michele?

Being with her had changed him.

Despite the paparazzi interrupting his and Michele's last kiss on the sand, he felt like he'd become a new man overnight.

He'd never found a woman he could talk to like her. Hell, he'd told her things he'd been afraid to admit to himself. Yet she hadn't run, hadn't judged. And she'd touched him like no one ever had—with reverence, kindness, and heat that had rocked him to the core.

Damn, they had sizzling chemistry. Even though he hadn't slept the entire night and had to get his head into the job at the restaurant site, he was still aroused thinking about their time on the beach. He wanted her now.

He slipped a note under her door.

"Please join me for dinner tonight. Yes, it's another date. Say yes."

He couldn't wait to see her naked again and drive deep inside her—maybe in his shower and then in his bed. Maybe twice in his bed.

At dinnertime, he called it a day at the building site and headed back to the house to find Michele. Since the chef competition was over, Donna and the rest of the cooking staff had come back to work. He was happy to see them, but a little disappointed that Michele wasn't in the kitchen. He'd grown accustomed to seeing her sweet face screwed up in concentration as she cooked. Not to mention her cute ass bending over the oven.

He was getting hard just thinking about her.

Only one thing to do…bound down the hall, take her in his arms and show her how much he'd missed her. When he got to her room, she was talking on her phone and sitting on a lounge chair on the balcony. The setting sun framed her in golden light and the ocean breeze lifted her long hair. He watched her stare out over the gardens.

God, she was stunning. His heartbeat sped up and there was a strange warmth filling him. He'd never felt anything like that before. It both scared and awed him.

"Yes, I see why you were in total lust with Jeffrey Harper," she laughed. "I get it. Boy, do I get it."

He grinned. She was talking about him, huh? He liked that more than he dared admit. Would she talk about his blue eyes, his red hair or his six-pack? Those were the three things most articles mentioned about him.

"He's a good man," she said.

Her words stunned him like a flash of sunlight on a black day. No one had ever called him a good man before and hearing it from her lips melted something hard that had been lodged in his chest. It also worried the hell out of him.

He wanted to be the man Michele thought he was. But there wasn't anything good about him. That wasn't going to change. He'd sleep with her for a while, make sure she had a good time, but then he'd have to follow through with his promise to his dad and find a wife.

The idea didn't sit well with him anymore.

"It happened fast, but yes," she went on softly. "I'm falling for him."

Warning bells rang in every part of his psyche.

She can't be in love with me.

Michele went on, "Please, don't let Cari see the picture of us at the dinner party. She'll think I'm marrying him and that's not going to happen. We want different things."

That knocked him back.

Michele didn't believe they had a future together, either. It was the truth. He needed to marry someone he couldn't hurt.

So why did her words sting so damned much? He turned around and walked away.

Michele was disappointed when Jeff hadn't come to collect her for dinner last night. One of the staff had dropped off a note that said Jeff had work to do and she should eat without him. He seemed to be extremely busy working on the restaurant.

The next morning, still dreaming about that beach encounter, she went into the kitchen and found the regular staff in place. She smiled and introduced herself to them. When an older woman with white hair named Donna stepped forward to shake her hand, Michele hugged her instead.

"Thank you for taking care of Jeff," she whispered in Donna's ear. "He told me about the shed."

Donna pulled back with wide eyes. "He told you?"

Michele nodded. "The secret is safe with me."

"Oh, sweet girl. Jeff has needed someone like you his entire life." Donna pulled Michele into a huge bear hug.

They nodded at each other, insta-friends.

"What can I make you?" Donna asked.

"Actually, I was hoping I could jump in here with you

and make a lunch for Jeff." Her brain was overflowing with recipes. Her cooking muse was back.

"Of course! He'd love that."

"I won't get in your way. I'm leaving in a few days anyway."

"What? No, you can't go."

"I've got to go back to New York to collect my things, pay rent and figure out how to bring my sister to California. But I want to do something nice for Jeff before I go."

"Sure, hon. My kitchen is your kitchen."

Later, Michele went down to the job site. The framing was finished. The restaurant seemed to be coming along faster than Jeff had said it would. It made her realize that she had a lot to do to be ready for opening night. She'd ask Donna if she could use Casa Larga's kitchen to create new recipes for the restaurant. Her brain was bubbling over with ideas.

Jeff came out of the building. He wasn't smiling and he didn't come close enough to touch.

Why the distance?

"Michele, what are you doing here?"

"I brought you lunch."

"That wasn't necessary."

She frowned. His vibe was all wrong. Was he mad at her?

"I know. I wanted to…" *See you. Touch you. Kiss you.* "…feed you. That's all."

He took the bundle from her hands. "Thanks."

She stood there, wondering what was going on with him. "So…"

He waited.

Okay, then.

He was busy or in a bad mood. She rushed on. "I won't take up any more of your time. I just wanted to know if I could go home for a couple of weeks to check on my sister. I miss her terribly. You know, if there was one thing I could change it would be to have her live with me. She needs round-the-clock care but I am sure there must be group homes in California, even if I have to drive a ways to get there."

She saw a subtle shift in his demeanor, a softening. But it passed quickly. He crossed his arms over his chest, closing himself off. "Fine. Distance between us is probably a good thing right now."

She blinked. "Jeff, what's the matter?"

He stepped closer and she could feel the intensity rising off his body in waves. "You can't love me, Michele. I won't allow it."

Her mouth opened. "Excuse me?"

"I told you. I'm broken, just like my mother. I sure as hell don't want to hurt you, of all people. God, Michele, you're special. Sweet. The gentlest person I've ever met. It'll kill me to cause you any pain. That's why we should stop seeing one another, except professionally."

You can't love me. She didn't know how he'd known, but it was the truth. She was starting to fall for him.

She couldn't help it.

"Jeff…" She reached for him but stopped, not wanting to see him recoil from her touch. "Maybe if we give it a little time—"

"I'm almost out of time."

"What do you mean?"

Instead of answering her question, he said, "Go home and see your sister. I'll give you three weeks to decide if you still want to work for me, knowing that I have to marry someone else."

Her heart broke. "You have to? Or want to?"

"It's not my choice. My father has made it part of my work contract. I have to marry someone when the restaurant is finished."

If her jaw could have hit the dirt, she would be tripping over it. "That's...months away."

The muscles in his jaw flexed. "I keep hoping I can change his mind, but he's a stubborn bastard."

None of this seemed real. He'd slept with her knowing he would be marrying someone else? "Who...?"

He lifted his hands. "I haven't found a bride yet."

"This is crazy! Your father can't make you do this."

"He can. I promised I would abide by the contract. I signed it." He exhaled through his nose. "Listen, I'm sorry. Not for what we had, that was amazing, but I can't get you messed up in my family drama, because you are too important to me."

"As your chef," she clarified.

"And I hope as a friend. But I leave the decision up to you. Think about it while you are in New York. If you don't want the job, I'll call Freja. I never wanted to hurt you."

He turned and walked away.

The kitchen stoves and appliances arrived that same day.

Jeff was busy directing the installations and didn't think about Michele, much. But when the sun went down and he had to eat dinner alone, their discussion weighed on him. The hurt look when he told her he was still marrying someone else tore him up, especially knowing that he'd put that sadness on her beautiful face. He cared about her, more than he should. Letting her go was for her own good. Once she was in New York she'd see he was lousy boyfriend material. She deserved so much more.

God, he should've chosen Freja for his chef. At least then he wouldn't torture himself every time he stepped into the kitchen. He wasn't good about abstaining from treats he couldn't have. Not being able to kiss Michele would be hard. That is *if* she decided to return. For her own good she should never return. But for *his* good? He still wanted her beside him. What a selfish bastard he was.

Even now he wanted to see her, touch her, inhale her sweet perfume. He went to find her to apologize for being so harsh earlier and beg her to stay. But he found her room empty. She'd already left.

What if she didn't come back? Had he lost his best chef? The only woman he'd ever cared about?

This was RW's fault. Dad was the one making Jeff get married. If he didn't have that stupid cloud over his head, he could date Michele and not worry about the future. They could simply enjoy one another for a while. Be together for as long as it lasted.

He didn't want to think about his own role in creating this heartache.

He stomped into RW's wing determined to make his father change his demands. He passed the guard and stepped into a dark hallway.

"Dad?" he called. "You in here?"

No answer. Frowning, Jeff turned on the hallway lights and knocked on RW's door. Music was playing inside. A strange foreboding came over him. Something wasn't right. He opened the door and stepped into total blackness. He fumbled around to find the light switch and was startled to see his father sitting at his desk drinking bourbon while a Mexican song blasted.

His father didn't drink. As far as Jeff knew, he didn't speak Spanish.

What the hell was going on?

"Dad? What's wrong?"

"Angel left. She took Cristina and the boy and drove away. How can I stay here and…breathe? I can't do this, any of it, without her. She was the only person who saw past this…" RW slapped his own chest "…this stupid man."

Jeff had never heard so much pain in his father's voice, in anyone's voice. "Where did she go? Is she all right?"

The look in his father's eyes was heart wrenching. It reminded him of the pain he'd been pushing past since he'd ended things with Michele.

"I don't know. How can I protect her when she won't let me? She said she couldn't put me at risk. Me! As if I wasn't dead before she started treating me."

Jeff ran his hand through his hair. "Let's go after her."

"No, dammit! Cuchillo will expect me to follow her. It's too risky." He grabbed Jeff's collar. "Swear you won't go after her."

Jeff gripped his father's wrist. "Fine. We'll wait for her to contact you."

"I'm not a patient man."

Jeff snorted. "Yeah, I know. But unless you have a better plan…"

RW shook his head and lifted the bottle to his lips.

Jeff pulled it away. "That's not helping. You stopped drinking, remember?"

"For Angel. She told me I couldn't see what was right in front of me from the bottom of a bottle. But without her… I lost my family and now my…angel. I'm alone." RW slumped over his desk.

"You're not alone. I won't leave you." Jeff hoisted RW up from under his arms. "Come on, Dad. Let's walk it off."

The next morning, Jeff woke up and cracked his back. He'd had a lousy night's sleep in the chair beside his father's bed. But at least his father's problems had kept Jeff's mind from lingering on Michele.

RW opened his eyes and cursed, gripping his head. Jeff handed him two aspirin and a bottle of water.

"Glad Angel isn't here to see me like this," RW said, his voice gravelly.

Jeff shrugged. "One bad night. Put it behind you and do better."

RW lifted his lips in a half grin, half grimace. "You sound like her. Of you three kids, she worried about you the most."

"Angel worried about me? Why?"

"Chloe told us about what your mother did to you in the shed and Matt told us that you worry you can never fall in love."

Jeff bolted up. "What the hell? You all sat around talking about me behind my back?"

"To help you, son. That's what families do." RW rose, too, swayed a little and put his hands on Jeff's shoulders. "I swear, I didn't know your mother left you out in the shed."

When RW grimaced that time, Jeff wondered if it was hangover pain or from imagining what his little boy had gone through. Part of him wanted his father to feel real pain. A white-hot poker of justice.

Something to block out his own pain over mistakes made.

"Bullshit. How could you not know how she was? Why didn't you stop her, Dad?"

RW nodded. "You're right. I should've been there to save you. It was my fault, Jeffrey. That's another thing on me that I need to make amends for, a bad one. Give me the blame and let your shame go."

Weakness seeped into Jeff's legs. "I need to sit down." He'd never heard his father accept the blame so quickly, and then apologize. It knocked him back, and he crumpled into the chair.

"Listen to me, son. You're nothing like your mother. You are ambitious, thick-skinned and strong. That's why your mother took her anger out on you. Not because you're like her, but because you are like me. She probably didn't even know that's why she picked on you so much."

Jeff blinked. RW had never been this open with him before.

"Another thing, I know you think your mother was incapable of loving. That's bull. Your mother loved me until I got sick. Something broke inside me and I couldn't love her anymore. I got mean and hurt her, too. Together, we raged World War Three on one another and destroyed…everything. I was too deep in my own hole to understand at the time, but I see now. Angel showed me the light."

Jeff hung his head between his knees. His limbs were heavy. "I don't know what to say."

"Say you're done hiding from your own damned feelings. Your mother and I hurt you badly and you don't want to hurt like that again. I get it. Trust me, I do, because you are like your old man. But if you don't let yourself feel, you'll never truly live. I want you to live, son."

And then, without any warning, RW wrapped his arms around Jeff.

For the first time in his life, Jeff buried his head in his father's shoulder and held on.

Eighteen

Michele flew to New York like a regular person—no chartered jet, yacht or limo. It was strange to be in New York again. Nothing had changed, except her. Days passed and she still felt out of place in her own home.

During the day, she stayed with her sister and answered the hundreds of questions that Cari's caregivers asked about the Harpers. They all wanted to know what Jeff was like in real life. The more Michele talked about him, the more she missed him. It was a sweet ache that wouldn't go away.

Did he think about her?

When she was back in her tiny apartment, she whipped up recipes one after the other. She kept a pad of paper on the countertop and by her bed so she could write down the rainbow of flavors that fired inside her brain.

Joy. That's what it felt like. Her cooking anxiety was gone.

So, apparently, was Alfieri's voice. Cooking for Jeff had silenced the negativity inside her.

She was free.

Man, she couldn't wait to create some of these dishes for Jeff. He'd love her mildly spicy chicken parmigiana. She smiled, thinking about how much he'd loved the grilled cheese sandwich she'd made for him. That was the first time she'd kissed his spicy lips and he'd asked her to eat with him.

Who was eating dinner with him now?

A horrible thought stopped her pen—what if he was married by the time she returned? Could she work for him then? She honestly didn't know if she could. It would hurt too badly. Her pain would be bad enough but watching him self-destruct with a person who didn't care about him, who maybe only wanted his money or fame? She couldn't bear the thought.

A friend. That's what he said he wanted her to be. Would a friend let him do something that would end up harming him?

No, she had to stop him from marrying a woman who would not love him. Because, heaven help her, *she* loved him. Desperately. Without question. She'd never loved a man before but she understood that love was about risks and she was willing to risk it all for Jeffrey Harper. She wanted him to be happy. She wanted to make the rest of his life sweeter than he could ever imagine. To do that…she would have to be brave and go for what she wanted—him.

Biting her lip, she knew what she had to do.

She called him and was disappointed when his voice mail picked up. How she'd wanted to hear his deep voice.

"It's Michele. If you still must get married…" Screwing up all the courage she could muster, she said, "Marry me. We're good together. Really good. Friends with benefits. I want you to be happy and I can make you happy. I know what I'm getting into. Please, call me back and we can…" she laughed "…plan a wedding. Call me."

She hung up and stared at her phone. Did she just ask a man to marry her?

Falling back on her bed she laughed out loud. Yes, she did.

Jeff was busier than he'd ever been but he couldn't stop thinking about Michele.

Would she come back?

And if she did, would he be able to keep his hands off her? He didn't think so. All he'd thought about, dreamed of, imagined since she left was Michele. He was glad he didn't have his cell phone with him at the site. He couldn't stop checking social media or searching the web for pictures of her. When he found nothing, the hole in his heart widened. He turned his phone off and buried it in his sock drawer.

RW showed up at the building site, looking ragged and drawn. Like a strong California sundowner wind would blow him off his feet.

"Hey, Dad. Have you heard from Angel yet?"

RW shook his head. The muscles in his jaw flexed. "I'm working another angle so she feels safe to come back once and for all."

Alarms went off in Jeff's head. "What sort of angle?"

"Taking the fight straight to the bastard himself. Cuchillo invaded my home. Now he'll see what that feels like."

Jeff didn't like the sound of this plan. "Ah, that sounds dangerous. I'm not sure you're up to that sort of fight, Dad."

The flash of fury in his father's eyes startled him. "I'm exactly the one for this fight. He hurt Angel and will pay for that. Don't worry, I'll make sure our family is protected."

Now Jeff was thoroughly worried. He would talk to Matt and figure out what the old man was planning.

"Dad…"

"I'm done discussing this." RW ended the conversation by walking around the building to check out the progress. Typical Dad move—walk away when he didn't want to hear any more.

Matt and I will figure it out.

Jeff continued working. It was all he could do with so much on his mind.

When RW reappeared ten minutes later, he said, "It's coming along."

"Yep. The kitchen will be fully functioning by the end of the week. Just have the rest of the dining area to finish up."

It was the first time he'd seen RW smile since Angel left. "I'm proud of you, son. This project is just what we both needed."

Warmth spread inside Jeff's chest. "Thanks, Dad."

"I haven't seen anything online from Finn lately." RW frowned. "I wonder what he's up to."

"Maybe our lawyers scared him off."

"Doubtful. I'll check into that, too. Okay, son. I'll leave you to your work."

Jeff watched his father walk away and wondered what *he* was up to.

* * *

Almost two weeks had passed since Michele left. It felt like a thousand. When was she coming back? Would she? The questions haunted him night and day. Jeff and Matt were insulting each other and playing an extremely aggressive game of pool when RW stomped into the pool house waving a newspaper. "What in the hell is this!"

Chloe rushed in behind him. "Dad, some of those go back to the start of the year before Jeff came home."

Jeff walked around the pool table to see what they were looking at. The headline read, "Jeffrey Harper's Harem." Below that were two pages filled with pictures of him on dates.

"No way. Are those women you've dated *this* year?"

Chloe bit her lip. "I have our image guys on it. But I'm not sure what they can do to help you, Jeff. These appear to be real pictures."

Matt cocked his head. "Oh, look, there's Michele Cox. And there she is again at the beach."

Jeff pressed his fingertips to his temple. "Finn did this."

Chloe nodded. "Sounds like something he'd do."

"I don't care who took the pictures. I've already gotten angry calls from shareholders. You're supposed to be building a respectable image, Jeffrey. Not—" RW slapped the page "—a harem."

"You told me to find a bride!" Jeff yelled.

"I didn't tell you to date every female in the northern hemisphere. You're sabotaging your career and hurting the family in the process. It's time to choose. Marry one," RW ordered.

Jeff wasn't ready to discuss it. He didn't know when he'd ever be ready to marry.

The only woman he'd made love to recently was Michele. She saw through the television celebrity image, the rich Harper prince, the cocky hotel critic, and saw the real him. Messed up childhood and all.

No one else got him like she did.

He didn't want to think about what that meant.

"What are we going to do about Finn?" Jeff asked instead.

"Leave him to me. I'll settle the score but we need him to come here. I can't go to New York, in case Angel needs me here. Plus, I'm working on something."

Jeff and Matt exchanged looks. So far, they hadn't figured out what RW was planning to do to Cuchillo.

Chloe studied RW's face. "How will you get Finn here?"

"I'll invite him to come see how the restaurant is coming along. Jeff, make sure your chef is ready to make him a meal he will never forget."

"When? Michele is not due back for another ten days." Jeff's gaze went to her picture. The one on the beach was his favorite. He traced her jaw with his finger.

"Michele Cox is not coming back. She tendered her letter of resignation this morning. To me," RW said.

Jeff turned around so quickly that the room spun. A low hum of despair started at the base of his tailbone. "She quit?"

"That's what happens when you let people down. She called you several times and you refused to call her back. Don't you understand what I am trying to teach you with this project?" RW's voice was raised but there was a thick undercurrent of sadness in it. "The towns-people. Our employees. People we care about. Harpers don't get to crap on anyone anymore. You lose good people that way…for good. I expect better of you."

Jeff slammed his hand on the pool table. "I didn't get her calls, Dad."

"Jeff, I bought you a new phone. Is it not working?"

"It's fine. It's just…my phone is… I turned it off. Social media was destroying me." He didn't explain that it was more the lack of seeing Michele anywhere than seeing his negative posts that were killing him.

Chloe said. "Did you bury it in your sock drawer like you used to?"

"Hey. How did you know I hid things there?"

Chloe smiled. "You're still the same. You know that? You always hid the good stuff there. Candy bars, comic books… I'll go get the phone."

Matt patted his shoulder. "Explain it to Michele. It's just a misunderstanding."

"Is it?" RW's nostrils flared. "Did you treat her badly, son? Could she have seen this two-page spread this morning and decided she didn't want to be another notch on your bedpost?"

Jeff opened his mouth. No words came out.

"If you want to be respected, you have to treat people with respect. Why can't you learn from my mistakes instead of making the same ones? This is yours to fix. Figure it out." RW stomped out the same way he came in.

Matt shook his head. "We really need to find Angel. Are you okay?"

No.

His mind was spinning, searching for answers. Jeff scrubbed his face.

She quit?

He'd really thought she'd come back, even if they couldn't be together anymore.

"I'm fine." His voice was full of gravel.

Matt rubbed his shoulder. "Of course, you are. Hey, you know what's different in these pictures? I just figured it out."

"You're still looking at those? Give it a rest."

Was Dad right? Had Michele seen this, too? Did she feel like just another woman in his bed? Hell, he could see her sparkle even in the grainy black-and-white shots. Could feel her touch way down deep.

She was nothing like the others.

"No way. Look. This is too good to pass up." Matt sounded amused.

Jeff didn't want to look. He'd forgotten many of their names already.

"It's a bunch of women I dated, so what?" Jeff snarled.

"No, jackass. Look at *you* in the pictures. Here's your ugly mug with all these women. Serious, glum, bored, practicing your multiplication tables in your head…" He pointed across two rows. "Now look at you with Michele. Both pictures. See the difference?"

Jeff leaned in closer. "I'm smiling at her."

"Bingo. A real smile, man. Like you feel it down to your toes. You are into her, totally and completely. At least, that's what I see in those two photos and not in the others. Hell, if I didn't know better, I'd say that guy in those two pictures with Michele—" Matt grinned. "That dude is in love."

Jeff looked closer and saw what Matt recognized.

He seemed like a different person in the photos with Michele. A person he'd never seen before.

He *was* different with Michele.

A surge of heat flooded his gut. It wasn't love, it was…hell, he didn't know what to call it. But it was…something.

Chloe raced in, out of breath, and shoved the shiny new phone toward him. "Here. Play the voicemails and call her right now. Tell her…tell her anything, something. She's good for you. Get her back, Jeff."

He stepped away from them and listened to the messages. All ten of them.

The air was sledgehammered out of his body. He slumped onto a bar stool and listened. A lump was in his throat when he closed the cell phone and faced his brother and sister.

"Matt, can you fly me to New York tonight?" he asked.

Matt raised his fist to the air. "Hell, yeah! Let's go get her."

"No. I have a score to settle with an asshole named Alfieri. That's all."

Chloe's eyes were full of concern. "What did Michele say?"

He swallowed but the damned lump wouldn't move. "She asked me to marry her. A few times. Eight, I think. Then waited for my answer. When I didn't call, she told me she never wanted to see me again. Another man had stolen her joy once, and she wasn't going to go through that again."

Matt sucked in a hiss of breath. "Go talk to her, bro. You can fix this."

The heat in Jeff's gut begged him to race after her,

grab her, kiss her until she changed her mind and came home with him.

But his mind knew otherwise.

"She's right. I'd only break her beautiful sparkle. Crush her joy. I don't deserve her."

Matt made a half grunt and used one of his little boy's catchphrases. "No, duh."

"Matt!" Chloe slapped Matt's arm.

"What? He *doesn't* deserve her. That's a given. We Harper men are totally screwed up. But here's the thing…" Matt wrapped his arm over Jeff's shoulder. "The right woman can make you a better man. I'm proof. I wake up every damned day amazed that Julia sees anything in me and go to bed praying, begging, that she never stops. Without her, I'm nothing. With her, I'm Matt on steroids, a flipping superhero." His grin was full of awe. "With all the powers."

"Go to her," Chloe said. "Love her, Jeff."

He couldn't. He didn't know how.

Nineteen

Michele was moving on. That's what she told herself.

What choice did she have, since there was no going back?

She'd laid it all on the line for him, and he hadn't even called her back to blow her off.

She owed Jeff a lot for helping her to see clearly and get her cooking mojo back. He'd taught her that she didn't need any man to tell her who she was. Michele Cox was still a kick-ass chef. The voice in her head was her own. She was small, but she was also mighty, and she had the power to take care of herself and her sister now.

She was alone, yes, but she didn't have time to dwell on it because she had three good job offers already. She would decide which one to take by the end of the week. Her goal now was to save enough money to start a restaurant of her own. A small one. Nothing like the posh restaurant Jeff was going to have, but it would be great. It would be hers. Stickerino's, she might call it—after the horse who carried the heroine to the pirate's treasure.

How she wished she could have kept the pirate as her treasure.

But he didn't want her, or at least, not enough.

So, she was moving on and she would stop thinking about *him*.

Eventually.

That was her plan anyway, until that two-page newspaper article hit all the stands with two pictures of her kissing Jeffrey Harper and her short-lived romance became the topic of conversation everywhere she went.

And the paparazzi found out where Cari lived.

Jeff had intended to come to New York for Alfieri, and Alfieri alone. He hadn't planned on seeing Michele, but now he had to. Because he had her money in his pocket and had a question to ask her.

Or that's what he told himself.

About seventeen times.

But his insides were thrumming with heat and excitement at the thought of seeing her again. *Just to give her the money and ask her the question*, he reminded himself for time number eighteen.

He didn't dare get too carried away. She probably hated him for not calling back after her emotional, heartfelt messages. And he knew he'd done the right thing by letting her go.

And yet, he still wanted to kiss her.

When he pulled up in front of her flat he couldn't help but notice the photographers. They were like a committee of hungry buzzards waiting outside. She didn't appear to be home. Good. He pulled up directions to the group home where he'd paid her sister's rent and sped off.

Dammit, reporters were parked outside the group home, too. Why in the hell were they bothering Michele's sister? Putting on a baseball cap, he walked inside.

The attendant at the front desk looked up warily. "Can I help you?"

"Hope so. I'm looking for Michele Cox."

When she saw who he was she squealed and then told him he'd just missed her. Michele had taken her sister to horseback riding lessons. The woman gave him the directions.

The vultures had beaten him to the stables, too. Police had been called and they and the stable owner were pushing the photographers off the private property. When an officer asked him what business he had at the stable, he said he was there to pick up one of the riders—a woman with special needs and her sister.

"I'm the owner," a woman said. "I'll let you pass if you tell me the name of the rider you are here to pick up."

"Cari Cox," he replied. "Her sister is Michele."

The woman grimaced. "Oh, good. Michele must've texted you, too. I was just getting ready to call one of my stable boys to come back to work and go rescue them."

"Rescue them?"

"One of the photographers opened the gate and went into the ring to get a picture of Cari, which, as you probably can guess, didn't go over well. She doesn't like strangers. She started screaming, the horse spooked and ran out of the gate with Cari on its back. Michele ran after them and then she got injured—"

"Michele is injured?" His heart just about exploded in his chest. "Where is she?"

"She texted that she twisted her ankle and can't walk. She can't make it to where Cari's horse is because the terrain is steep."

"Where? Can I drive there?"

"No. Can you ride?"

"Yes."

"Then take my horse. She's saddled up and ready to go. I'd do it myself but I have to make sure these nut-balls don't sneak back onto my property—"

"Text Michele. Tell her to sit tight. I'm coming." He would fly if he had to. He stopped telling himself lies about why he'd come to New York because he needed to hold her and kiss her pain away.

"That was fun! Really fast. I was like Rosie," Cari squealed and giggled in delight.

"Sure, laugh. It's all fun and games until your sister nearly breaks a leg running after you."

"You dance funny."

That's because Michele had stepped in a hole and twisted her ankle. "I wasn't dancing."

Out of nowhere came the memory of Jeff's hands on her hips at the dinner party. Now those were real moves. She shook it off. She didn't have the time or the stamina to be heartsick. What did it matter that she missed him like crazy? He'd made his feelings clear by not returning her calls.

"Can you give your horse a little kick and steer him toward me? I can't hop on one foot that far. And this other one is…" She looked at her leg. It was terribly swollen already. Oh, God, was it broken? "It's not good."

"My horse likes the grass here. He's hungry."

"He gets plenty of food in the stables. Let's take him back there where he can have a proper dinner and I can get some ice for my leg, okay? Come over here so I can ride with you."

"No. You are too heavy. Only one cowgirl on each horse."

Michele cursed under her breath and tried hopping on one foot. It was no good. The path was rocky and steep. Cari's horse had found a grass-covered mesa at the top of the hill. How was she going to make it up there? Crawl?

"Ahoy, there. Need a lift?" A voice called behind her.

She couldn't see the man, but she was overjoyed that the owner had sent someone to rescue her and Cari.

"Yes! But please, don't spook my sister's horse."

It took a small feat of balance to be able to turn her body on one foot without slipping down the steep embankment. By the time she did, the horse and rider were already beside her.

"Did someone order a cowboy from California?" he asked.

She blinked. No. It couldn't be.

"You're not real."

He laughed then and her heart did funny things in her chest. "Tell that to my horse." He slid down and stood beside her. His starburst baby blues seemed to take her all in. "Are you hurt?"

She pressed a hand to her heart.

Oops, did he mean her ankle? "It might be broken."

He bent over and checked it out. When he touched

her leg, she bit her lip to keep it from quivering, not entirely from the twisted ankle pain either.

Jeff is here.

Why? What does it mean?

"I don't think it's broken, but you twisted it good. Let me help you up on the horse so we can have a doctor look at it. Do you want the front or rear seat?"

She realized there wasn't much room for him to sit behind the saddle. "Rear."

Once he got her situated on the horse, he swung his leg over and sat in front of her. She had a sudden dilemma. Should she touch him? For the moment, she kept her hands to herself.

"My sister is over there." Michele pointed. "She's pretending to not see you."

"I can see that. What am I supposed to do?"

"Cari, this is a friend of mine named Jeff. He's very nice," Michele called out.

"The pirate!" Cari clapped her hands.

Oh, dear. "Um. Yes." Michele leaned over and whispered. "Sorry. Someone must have mentioned your family history. Cari's favorite book has pirates in it."

He grinned. "So, Cari, how would you like to go with me and your sister on an airplane back to a pirate's castle?"

"Yay!" Cari cheered. "Right now?"

"What?" Michele said. "You can't just tell her things like that."

"Listen, sweetheart. It's not safe for you two to be here by yourselves right now. I saw the paparazzi. They're everywhere because of me. Let me fix it. If you aren't around here, they'll leave after a while."

"But, I have a life here. A job to accept."

"It will all still be here if you want it, but I was hoping you'd change your mind about the resignation and come back to Plunder Cove. For good. If…you'll accept my proposition. But first, let's go get your sister, okay?"

She stared at his back. *Proposition?*

"Okay?" he asked again.

"I…don't know what I'm agreeing to."

"Fair enough. Tiny bites. First, we rescue your sister and that fat horse."

"I agree."

"Great. But I'm not moving until you wrap your arms around me. Safety first."

Tentatively, slowly, she wrapped her arms around his waist. He took her hand and pressed it against his chest. Capturing it next to his heart. She could feel the strong beat beneath her palm. He felt so good in her arms, even when she knew he didn't feel the same way about her. Her heart was cracking from the bitter sweetness of it all. She wanted to stay like this forever, touching him, breathing in his manly cologne, listening to his deep voice. Holding out hope that he wouldn't say he didn't love her. Again.

"That's better." His voice was hoarse. "Hell, I missed you so hard. Please, say you'll come back with me."

Her inhale caught in her throat. The only word she could muster was, "Why?"

"I'm miserable without you. I still need a chef, and that job is still yours, but you deserve more. Which reminds me…" He reached into his pocket and pulled out a thick envelope that seemed to be full of…money? "This is yours. I had a little chat with Alfieri. He was overcome with the desire to pay you what he owed you. With interest, of course."

"That's…no. Now I know you're not real. I must have hit my head when I twisted my ankle."

"Does this feel real?" He lifted her hand and kissed her knuckle. Then he turned her hand over and kissed her palm. "Or this?"

"Yes," she said softly. She felt those kisses all the way down to her throbbing ankle. It was all she could do to not beg for more. "I'm so ashamed. I should never have let Alfieri treat me like that."

"Sorry, sweetheart, but that's pure bull." He swiveled around and pinned her with his gaze. "He assaulted you with his words and actions and robbed you. You have nothing to be ashamed of. I'm glad you got away from him and I told him so…in something like words."

"You didn't hurt him, did you?"

"Hell, I wanted to. But I think my old camera crew will hurt him far more than I could unless he agrees to change his ways. They'll pop in on him and interview the staff on a regular basis just to make sure he's a kinder, gentler Alfieri. So that he doesn't do to others what he did to you."

"Thank you."

"There's more. I found out he'd promised you a partnership in the restaurant and that's when the coincidence hit me. I need a partner in *my* restaurant while I build and run the hotel. Someone I trust. That's my proposition. Will you be my partner?"

She cleared her throat. "In the restaurant?"

"What do you think? We can get the finest care for your sister and you two can live together again. It's perfect."

Almost.

"What about your wedding plans?"

His shoulders stiffened. "RW may not like it, but if you agree to come back as my partner, I'll break my agreement with him."

"You won't get married?"

"No." He swiveled so she could see his face. He went on, "And you and I can focus on our careers. I can take care of you and your sister and together you and I can create the best restaurant the world has ever seen. Say yes."

"And we, the two of us, will be real partners? Nothing more?"

He stiffened again. "You are much more. You are important to me, Michele. I hope you see that. I don't want to jeopardize our...relationship, or our restaurant, in any way. I need you."

She sighed. He would never love her. "I see."

It wasn't the partnership she'd been hoping for—it wasn't the one she'd bet her heart on when she'd left him those voice messages—but she'd get to be with him and she'd be doing what she loved.

She'd spent too long without what she wanted and even if he never loved her back, she would take everything he'd give.

"I say yes."

She put her head on his back, breathed in his most excellent manly smell and took a second to notice all the places they were touching.

Just then Cari's horse decided to come down and join theirs.

"Weeeee!" Cari said. "Let's go to the pirate castle."

Twenty

The day arrived. Finn had been invited to Casa Larga to see the restaurant and taste some of Michele's new creations. RW knew the bastard would come. Finn owed him.

RW met him in the circle of the driveway. When Finn got out of the limo with a swagger, RW's blood boiled.

"Hello, old friend." Finn held out his hand.

RW took it and shook, but then he squeezed, dug his nails in and refused to let go until he had Finn's full attention. "You were only supposed to threaten him. Convince him to leave the television show and come to work for me. That was the deal."

Finn squinted and yanked his hand back. "It worked, didn't it?"

"I didn't tell you to attack my son," RW snarled.

Finn shrugged. "Attack him? I sent my best girl in

there. Jeffrey was the one who went ballistic. What in the hell is the matter with him?"

"Nothing," RW said.

The problem is mine.

All RW wanted was what was best for his son. Creating hotels was in Jeffrey's blood, in his heart. RW had done everything he could to convince Jeff to design the hotel at Plunder Cove, but that damned show, *Secrets and Sheets*, got in the way. RW had taken drastic measures to put an end to it by asking Finn to nudge Jeffrey in the right direction.

That had been a mistake.

RW was heartbroken to see that he'd been responsible for Jeffrey's internal struggles. It all stopped now.

"I want the videos and the photos to end. Hear me? You are done," RW said through gritted teeth.

"I hear nothing but hot air whistling in my ears, Harper. I'll stop when I have the episode he filmed of my hotel. That's my deal."

RW's hands clenched into fists. Rage pounded behind his eyeballs.

Chloe came out the front door, effectively ending the clandestine meeting. "Mr. Finn! Welcome. Please follow me to the restaurant. It is not finished yet, but the kitchen is fully functional and we have seating in the courtyard." She guided him to a comfortable table next to the firepit. "Enjoy!"

Jeff walked outside to the patio. "Finn, I can't say I am happy to see you."

There was a loud crash inside the unfinished restaurant. A drill, somewhere around the back of the site, made a horrible grinding sound followed by cussing.

The commotion made Finn grin. "Your restaurant is just as I imagined it."

"We're still getting the kinks out."

"I can only imagine that your hotel will be just as kinky." Finn picked up his cell. "I'm going to film this meal and Tweet it."

"Great." Jeff hoped Michele was ready. "Red or white wine?"

"A glass of each."

"Of course." It was a struggle not to grab the man by his collar and throw him out, but Dad had a plan—something he hadn't completely shared with his sons.

Imagine that.

Finn was working on both of his wine glasses when Michele softly called, "Order up."

Jeff picked up the plate. Michele had made her signature chicken cacciatore but the sauce was better than Alfieri's. Michele had fed him an early spoonful and he thought it was the best thing he'd ever tasted—next to Michele's lips. He missed her mouth and running his hands over her body.

Finn took a bite and rolled his eyes. Overwhelmed, he mumbled, "Holy crap. It's better than sex."

Jeff lifted his eyebrow and Michele nodded. They'd heard Finn all the way in the kitchen, since RW had bugged the table.

"Round two," Jeff said before he left the kitchen.

"Give him a knockout punch for me." Michele winked.

Damn, she was amazing.

Having her as his partner in the restaurant should've been a dream come true. She was the perfect, hardworking professional who created the best meals he'd ever eaten. If anything, she was too perfect, too dedicated. He was the one who had trouble focusing with her so near. He longed to sweep her away and find quiet moments for just the two of them. But he didn't, because they'd made a deal and he was determined to hold up his end of it. No matter how much he hated it.

A professional relationship with Michele wasn't enough. For the first time in his life, he wanted more. Something big was pounding inside him, burning to get out, struggling to have a voice to tell her what he probably knew all along—he wanted Michele. Forever.

He doubted she'd ever want him. Not after he'd let her walk away. He should have fought for her, begged her to stay in his life, instead of offering her a simple partnership. It wasn't enough. He'd blown it.

To Finn, Jeff said, "How's it going? More water? Another bottle?"

"More food. This is the best damned meal I've ever had." Finn shook his head, his eyes already having trouble focusing. "You did something right. Your chef is brilliant."

"I agree. But she is more than a chef. She's my partner. The best part of me." He hoped she heard that.

"Bully for you. What's for dessert?"

"Get ready, because Michele's tiramisu is the best, sweetest thing you will ever taste. She has her own secret spices from Italy plus a rare organic cocoa from a small farm in Ghana. You will swear you have died and gone to heaven."

"Enough jaw-flapping, Harper. Bring it on!"

Absolutely, you arrogant prick.

He went back into the kitchen. He'd done his job

sparring with the man; it was time to let his dad deliver the final blow.

RW sat at the table across from Finn. "Enjoying your meal?"

"I have never tasted anything like it. Such a pleasurable surprise. Where did you find your chef?"

"Jeffrey found her, not me. But I'm going to tell her not to serve you anything else unless you stop releasing clips from Jeffrey's sex tape."

Finn snorted. "You call *that* a sex tape?"

"What would you call it?"

"I don't know. A Photoshop masterpiece? It's flawless. I dare you to find anyone who can tell where I sliced the sections together."

"What about the woman? Is she really a maid?"

"No. She's one of my best hookers. Gorgeous tits. Sweet ass. She really brings in the dough, so I only charge her a small referral fee."

"Pimp commission, you mean."

Finn sipped his wine. "Tomato, tomato."

Listening in the kitchen, Michele sucked in a breath. "Did you know Finn ran a brothel in his hotel? "

"Some of the employees I interviewed hinted at something going on behind the scenes," Jeff said. "He's a real creep."

"And he made it look like you had the sex issues! I can think of stronger words than 'creep.'"

They continued to eavesdrop on the conversation outside.

"Interesting discussion," RW said. "So now that I've fed you a great meal by Chef Michele Cox and let you be the first to experience this amazing up-and-coming

Plunder Cove restaurant and hotel, I want to ask you nicely to stop blackmailing my son."

Finn shrugged. "No can do. I haven't gotten what I want yet. Wait until you see what I do with the next segment of video. With a little cut and splice wizardry, the world is going to think your son is one twisted sucker."

"Why are you doing this?" RW growled.

"You know why. He still hasn't televised how fantastic my hotel is. I need people to believe it's perfect. There's a lawsuit breathing down my neck."

"You want Jeffrey to lie to the public."

"Well, damn, RW, I can't have Jeffrey telling the truth! I watched what he filmed on my own security cameras. That episode would bury my hotel. I'd be run out of New York. That's why I had to create the fake sex tape. Your son has too damned much integrity to be pressured into turning over that episode. He wouldn't listen to reason."

RW crossed his arms. "And that's where he and I differ. Integrity? Not so much. Fierce determination to protect what's mine? You haven't seen anything like me. Guards! Take this scumbag off my property."

Finn laughed. "Right. Good one. Where's my tiramisu?"

RW picked up the tiny camera stuck to the flowerpot. And pointed to the recording device on the bottle of wine. There was another one under the table and a third one under his chair. "Seems like you are the one caught on tape, Xander. It's going to be a great commercial for the restaurant."

"You wouldn't dare."

"I'm releasing the part where you talk up the food. That's good stuff. If I see even one more shot, video, GIF—*anything*—on the internet about Jeffrey, I don't

care who posts it, I'll release the entire video shot tonight to the press. All of it. Understand me?"

"But…" Finn sputtered. "I thought we had a deal."

"We do now. Good luck, Xander. Do not cross me."

Michele stood in the kitchen beside Jeff, listening
to every word. When Finn started demanding his dessert, she fed it to Jeff bite by bite. She had absolutely
no intention of giving anything more to that vile Finn.

He'd blackmailed the man she loved to try to force
him into lying. How preposterous was that? Jeff didn't
lie.

"Holy sweetness, Batman. This is amazing," Jeff
said with his mouth full.

"Catwoman. I had the costume and everything."

He cocked his eyebrow. "Babe, I'd love to see you
in that costume." He waggled his finger for her to feed
him more. With each spoonful, his eyes rolled back in
pure delight. The look did wicked things to her. How
she wished they were still dating.

When they heard the guards throwing Finn off the
property, Jeff said, "I don't need to have my producer
give me the Finn hotel episode now. Finn just sealed
his own fate."

Michele cheered, "We did it!" And jumped into his
arms.

The kisses on his cheeks, jaw, neck and lips? Well,
she couldn't stop them if she tried.

And she hadn't tried.

Somewhere in the back of her mind, she sensed that
it was a mistake. They had a deal to be partners only
and she'd kept her side of it until tonight. But his lips
were an intoxicating mix of dark chocolate, cinnamon

and rum. Everything began to spiral out of control. His hands dove into her hair and held her head as they devoured each other's lips.

God, he tasted and felt so good.

She barely registered that he'd sat her down on the counter. All her thoughts were centered on this man. His tongue plunged inside her mouth. His hands roughly grabbed her butt.

She wanted more, needed more. Wrapping her legs around him, she pulled him closer until she could feel his thick erection pressing against her panties.

"Michele." The way he growled her name melted her.

If this was a mistake, she was going to make it big-time.

He was hard and she was desperate. She ground herself against his zipper. "Please," she begged. "I need you."

His groan of desire made her wet.

He cupped her through her panties, pressing his thumb against her nub, and nearly short-circuited her brain. She tossed her head back and arched as he rubbed in circles. Panting, she was in a frenzy to get him inside her.

She wanted to come with him. Biting her lip, she unzipped his pants.

His eyes were blue pools of hot desire. "Condom." He yanked his wallet out of his back pocket and took out a silver packet. When he was ready, he lowered her until he filled her.

This. Was. Perfect.

He started thrusting and she held on to his shoulders, rolling with him. Taking him in as deep as she could. "Michele." That growl again.

With each thrust, he said her name, never breaking eye contact. "My Michele."

He took her higher and higher until her body screamed for release and yet she tried to hang on so they could come together because she'd wanted him for what felt like forever. She needed this one moment to last for as long as she could stretch it out and save each second of it in her memory. She'd keep it locked away in her cracked heart, safe, perfect for the times when she was lonely. Alone. Love with Jeff was beautiful and so hard. It broke her even now as she knew he'd pull away again, needing to push her out of his arms because he couldn't feel what she did. He didn't know how to let himself fall for her.

"Sweet Michele," he said with a contented sigh against her neck. He was spent. She let herself sail away with him.

A few minutes later he said, "Don't move."

Move? How could she? Her body was a puddle of happy pudding.

He disposed of the condom and came back to wrap his arms around her. Against her neck he said, "One of these days, I want to take my time with you. Go slow."

Tears pricked her eyes. He was thinking of a future with her. "Slow, fast, I'll take you any way I can get you." She still meant it. She'd risked it all over and over for him, and she'd do it again. There was only one thing she craved in return—his whole heart.

Her body pulsed with her need for Jeffrey Harper and because she couldn't contain her emotions any longer, she let them out. "I want to be with you, Jeff." She loved him. Pure and simple.

"I'm right here, babe." He nuzzled her neck. She

sensed that he was distracting her, trying to steer her away from the discussion to come. He knew what she was going to say.

Her insides crumbled because she thought she knew what he was going to say, too, still she pressed on because she had to hear the words. "Are you? Or will you push me away again and tell yourself you can't have a real relationship?"

That's when she saw it—something sharp and raw twisted his beautiful face. He stepped back. "What do you want me to say?"

"The truth."

He swallowed hard, as if his throat was coated with sand. "I've always told you the truth."

"Not about your feelings. Those you shield, protect and bury deep. Say what you think about me, about us. Not what you worry we'll become but what we really are."

He shook his head, his blue eyes clouded. "I don't want to hurt you, Michele. I never did."

"The only way you'll hurt me is if you don't let yourself hang on to what is real and special, standing right here in front of you."

"Michele, this isn't easy for me." A thread of warning rumbled in his voice. He didn't want to talk about his feelings.

She couldn't stop now. "Remember when you said you wished you could feel something real? Feel this." She pressed his hand to her chest. Her heart was pounding hard. "Please, Jeff, I need you to see the man I see— an amazingly gorgeous guy who is worthy of love. Don't you see that, too?"

He didn't answer for a long moment. Tipping his head

toward the ceiling lights, he let out a deep exhale. She could tell he was struggling. "When I look at myself, I see a guy who has a restaurant that needs attention and a hotel to finish." He rubbed her arm, slowly, sensually. "Standing next to a beautiful and amazing chef who is going to put our restaurant on the map. I don't want to screw this up."

Damn. He just did.

She'd wanted to believe he cared for her so badly that she'd ripped her heart out of her own chest and handed it to a man who'd warned her he couldn't love her. She couldn't do this anymore.

A tear dripped down her cheek. "Being the head chef of a five-star restaurant isn't enough. I want more for you and need more for me. I wish you could see us like I do."

Until Jeff was brave enough to trust himself and her, she had to step away. She wouldn't give up the job she loved, but she needed to let the man she loved slip through her fingers. She had to let him go.

Everything hurt. It was almost as bad as the day Mom died. She couldn't breathe, but her legs, they could move. She fast-walked outside.

"Michele, wait!" he called after her.

She kept going because she didn't want to see him or hear any of his pretty words. Especially not the way he said her name. None of it was as real for him as it was for her. It never would be.

"Stop!" he called. "Please don't leave. I don't want to lose you."

She turned around and was surprised by the sadness she saw in his eyes and the tenseness of his jaw. "I'm not leaving. I love what we're creating together in the restaurant. I just… I can't date you anymore if you don't care about a real future with me. It's too painful."

He kneaded his neck, as if trying to release the tension she could see in his body. "I'm not any good at this, Michele. I've never been in a relationship before and I don't want to fail you. Hell, I wanted to protect you. From the press, my family, from me."

"From you?"

He stepped closer, his gaze boring into hers. "Yeah. I don't deserve you. I never did. But the truth is that I want you, Michele, more than I can say, more than I ever thought possible. I started crushing on you the first time I saw you on television cooking with such finesse and poetry in action. I've fallen hard every second after that." He wrapped his hands around her waist. "I'm not me— the real me—without you. Please, give me a chance to show you what I feel."

He pulled her to him and kissed her then and the whole world started spinning around her like she was flying. After several minutes he finally pulled back, pressed his forehead to hers and gazed into her eyes. "Did you feel that?" he asked. "I love you, Michele."

She blinked and tears sprang off her eyelashes. "You love me?"

"Hell, yes, with everything in me." His voice choked with emotion. "I'm a mess, sweetheart. I've never felt like this before." His words flowed out like the breaking of a dam. "This—you and me—it's intense. Consuming heat, burning need, but good, too. Warm and sweet. Your touch heals me. When you left, every part of me ached. I was ill with the need of you. Starved for your touch. The wanting of you tore me up inside. I love you so damned much that I can't think straight. I was afraid to admit it, afraid of who I'd become if I let you love me. I don't want to hurt you like my parents hurt each other."

Her heart was so full it hurt. "That won't happen because you are not them. You, Jeffrey Harper——" she held him as tightly as she could, their hearts pounding together "——are mine. We'll figure this all out together." She wrapped her hand around his neck and pulled his lips to hers.

When they finally came up for air she said, "I love you, too."

He exhaled. "Hell, that makes this next part easier." He linked his fingers with hers and kissed her wrist, sending shivers up her arm. "I had a whole thing planned out for tonight. Been working on it for days, but you sort of messed up my timing. Not that I'm complaining about how you preempted it."

"What thing?"

"Sunset yacht cruise up the coast to our beach. Bonfire. Champagne. This." He pulled a box out of his pocket.

She gasped.

He cupped her cheek with his big, warm hands. His gaze bored into her soul. "If you'll let me, I'll be the guy by your side, your partner in life. The one who encourages you and touches you as deeply as you touch me. I want to fall asleep to the rhythm of your breathing and wake up wrapped around you. You inspire me and make me laugh. You heal me and warm all the coldness inside. I want to do all those things for you and more. Much more. Let me be the man who makes *you* happy. Please let me love you for the rest of our lives.

I promise I'll get better at it. I'll talk to a therapist, do whatever it takes to get brave for you."

He dropped to his knee in the grass. "Michele Cox, will you marry me?"

She squealed, "Yes! Oh, Jeff, yes!" And then she dropped to her knees and kissed his spicy lips.

Epilogue

Epilogue

The small crowd filed in, taking their seats in chairs by the wedding pagoda at Seal Point—the place where Jeff and Michele had their first date under the canopy of stars. The waves crashed below and a mocking bird sang an artistic medley while Jeff snuck around the back of the restaurant to steal a peek at the bride.

Cari was in the doorway shifting her feet side-to-side, watching her dress swish with her movements.

"Hey, pretty lady. Where's your sister?"

"In there." Cari pointed to the dressing room. "Michele said you aren't supposed to look."

He grinned. "Aw, come on. Just a quick peek. Maybe a big old kiss."

Michele's voice came from somewhere inside. "Tell that sexy man out there to save his kisses until he says, 'I do.' And no peeking!"

Cari screwed up her face in confusion, trying to remember all the words. "She says, um..."

He pulled Cari into his arms. "I heard the bossy woman. I can give you a kiss on the cheek, though, right?"

"Yep. You're gonna be my big brother."

"Can't wait." When he kissed her cheek, Cari giggled. "Okay, tell my love to hurry up. I'm dying out here. She needs to come out and be my bride right now."

Chloe rounded the corner. "Get out of here! It's bad luck. And you don't want to smudge her lipstick. We just got it right." Then she kissed him on the cheek. "Love you. Now get up front."

"Fine. So many bossy women in here. I'm going."

"Jeff!" Michele called out.

He didn't stop to wonder why she'd called his name. She needed him and that was all that mattered. Screw bad luck. He ran past his sister and Cari and into the bridal room.

Gorgeous didn't begin to describe Michele. She was so beautiful that he couldn't breathe right and his lips felt wonky and his eyes were too full. His legs were full of sand.

"Do you still want to marry me?" Michele asked. "Now's your chance to call it off."

He forced his sand-filled legs to wobble toward her. Her eyes scoured his face, stopping on his lips. Did she see them trembling?

"Sweetheart, I have never wanted anything more. I love you, Michele. With all my heart. Please don't doubt that, but..."

Her lip started to tremble, too. "But?"

"You are so much better than me." He swallowed. "Do you really want to marry *me*?"

She let out a long breath. "Hell, yes."

He kissed her then and smudged her lipstick all over the place.

The wedding was running late, but he didn't care. He'd kissed his bride. All was well with the world.

When he was standing by the pagoda, butterflies of anticipation filled him. Michele was finally going to be his.

Matt bumped his elbow. "You've got this, bro. Just keep your eyes on her. She'll pull you through. I knew she was the one for you. Knew it all along."

RW nodded at him. "We all knew it."

Sure you did, old man.

Jeff took an extra moment to assess his father's demeanor. His eyes were clear, but there was still tightness around his mouth and eyes because Angel hadn't come home. No one knew where she was. Dad was dealing with it by "working the angles." Jeff was only starting to understand what that meant.

Matt had friends in the Bureau who'd slipped him intel that RW was working with the FBI to go after Cuchillo. That scared Matt but Jeff understood that a man would do what he had to do to protect his woman and bring her home safely. Besides, RW knew what he was doing. Jeff had a strong sense that the thing with Finn had started out as RW's devious plan to bring him home. The man was a scheming genius.

If Jeff hadn't met Michele, he'd be furious instead of grinning his fool head off right now.

The music started up and Jeff squinted to see the love of his life. If this wedding didn't happen soon he was going to combust. He was desperate to start his life as a married man with his sparkly bride. He was going to love her with everything he had and then learn how to love her even more.

Just then, a car roared up to the parking lot and the back door flew open. Jeff couldn't see who it was but he sensed the sudden tension in the air. Red heat covered RW's face and his eyes fired up with an intense, unnamed emotion. Matt's face was pale and his body rigid.

Who was it? Jeff still couldn't see.

A figure stepped out of the car, walking toward them with clipped, deliberate movements.

And then he knew.

"Oh, hell." Jeff turned to Matt. "Who invited Mom?"

* * * * *

RW's ex-wife has returned!
What will that mean for him and Angel?
Will he protect her from the gang that
will stop at nothing to find her?

And what will happen when
Chloe's role at the hotel puts her
face-to-face with a Brazilian pop star
who makes her want
all the things she shouldn't?

Don't miss the final story in the
Plunder Cove trilogy,
available July 2019!

COMING NEXT MONTH FROM

✦ HARLEQUIN®
Desire

Available March 5, 2019

#2647 HOT TEXAS NIGHTS
Texas Cattleman's Club: Houston
by Janice Maynard
Ethan was Aria's protector—until he backed away from being more than friends. Now her family is pressuring her into a marriage she doesn't want. Will a fake engagement with Ethan save the day? Only if he can keep his heart out of the bargain...

#2648 BOSS
by Katy Evans
I have a new boss—and he's hot but irresponsible, a youngest son. If he thinks he can march into this office and act like he owns the place, he needs to think again... If only I didn't want him as much as I hate him...

#2649 BILLIONAIRE COUNTRY
Billionaires and Babies • by Silver James
Pregnant and running from her almost in-laws, Zoe Parker is *done* with men, even ones as sinfully sexy as billionaire music producer Tucker Tate! But Tucker can't seem to let this damsel go—is it her talent he wants, or something more?

#2650 NASHVILLE SECRETS
Sons of Country • by Sheri WhiteFeather
For her sister, Mary agrees to seduce and destroy lawyer Brandon Talbot. He is, after all, the son of the country music star who ruined their mother. But the more she gets to know him, the more she wants him...and the more she doesn't know who to believe...

#2651 SIN CITY VOWS
Sin City Secrets • by Zuri Day
Lauren Hart is trying to *escape* trouble, not start *more*. But her boss's son, Christian Breedlove, is beyond sexy and totally off-limits. Or is he? Something's simmering between them, and the lines between work and play are about to blur...

#2652 SON OF SCANDAL
Savannah Sisters • by Dani Wade
At work, Ivy Harden is the perfect assistant for CEO Paxton McLemore. No one knows that she belongs to the family that has feuded with his for generations... until one forbidden night with her boss means *everything* will be revealed!

YOU CAN FIND MORE INFORMATION ON UPCOMING HARLEQUIN® TITLES, FREE EXCERPTS AND MORE AT WWW.HARLEQUIN.COM.

HDCNM0219

I have a new boss—and he's hot but irresponsible, a youngest son. If he thinks he can march into this office and act like he owns the place, he needs to think again... If only I didn't want him as much as I hate him...

Read on for a sneak peek of
Boss
by New York Times *bestselling author Katy Evans!*

My motto as a woman has always been simple: own every room you enter. This morning, when I walk into the offices of Cupid's Arrow, coffee in one hand and portfolio in the other, the click of my scarlet heels on the linoleum floor is sure to turn more than a few sleepy heads. My employees look up from their desks with nervous smiles. They know that on days like this I'm raring to go.

Though it sounds bigheaded, I know my ideas are always the best. There's a reason Cupid's Arrow swept me up at age twenty. There's a reason I'm the head of the department. I carry the design team entirely on my own back, and I deserve recognition for it.

The office doors swing open to reveal Alastair Walker—the CEO, and the one person I answer to around here.

"How's the morning slug going, my dear Alexandra?" he asks in that British accent he hasn't quite been able to shake off, even after living in Chicago for a decade. He's adjusting his sharp suit as he saunters into the room. For his age, he's a particularly handsome man, his gray hair and the soft creases of his face doing little to steal the limelight from his tanned skin and toned body.

At the sight of him, my coworkers quickly ease back.

"The slug is moving sluggishly, you might say," I admit, smiling in greeting.

When Alastair walks in, everyone in the room stands up straighter. I'm glad my team knows how to behave themselves when the boss of the boss is around. But my own smile falters when I notice the tall, dark-haired man falling into step beside Alastair.

A young man.

A very hot man.

He's in a crisp charcoal suit, haphazardly knotted red tie and gorgeous designer shoes, with recklessly disheveled hair and scruff along his jaw.

Our gazes meet. My mouth dries up.

And it's like the whole room shifts on its axis.

I head to my private office in the back and exhale, wondering why that sexy, coddled playboy is pushing buttons I was never really aware of before. Until now.

Don't miss what happens when Kit becomes the boss!
Boss
by Katy Evans.

Available March 2019 wherever
Harlequin® Desire books and ebooks are sold.

www.Harlequin.com